FAMILY

AN EXPLORATION

Betty Jane Wylie

FAMILY

AN EXPLORATION

Northstone

Editors: Michael Schwartzentruber, Dianne Greenslade
Cover and interior design: Margaret Kyle
Consulting art director: Robert MacDonald

Northstone Publishing Inc. is an employee-owned company, committed to caring for the environment and all creation. Northstone recycles, reuses and composts, and en-
courages readers to do the same. Resources are printed on
recycled paper and more environmentally friendly
groundwood papers (newsprint), whenever possible. The
trees used are replaced through donations to the Scoutrees
For Canada Program. Ten percent of all profit is donated
to charitable organizations.

Every effort has been made to acquire permission to re-
produce copyrighted material. Any oversights or omissions
will be corrected in future editions.

Small portions of this book have been previously published
in *All In The Family* (Key Porter, 1988).

Canadian Cataloguing in Publication Data
Wylie, Betty Jane, 1931-
    Family

    Includes bibliographical references and index.
    ISBN 1-896836-01-1

    1. Family. II. Family—Canada. I. Title
HQ560.W94 1997   306.8'0971   C96-910896-6

Published by Northstone Publishing Inc.

Printing 10 9 8 7 6 5 4 3 2 1
Printed in Canada by Friesen Printers

DEDICATION

To Judy Bager,
who has been a sister to me.

ACKNOWLEDGMENTS

I want to thank Robert Glossop of the Vanier Institute of the Family for his unfailing support and constant source of information and inspiration.

CONTENTS

PREFACE

Although Canadian families experience many problems, for better or worse, the majority of Canadian marriages do last for a lifetime.

Robert Glossop

Eighty-six percent of all young people aged 15 to 24 say they intend to have children.

Statistics Canada

People construct their families not only from the relationships within the family but also out of the elements from the society around them.

Dr. Frank Cassidy

Chances that an abused woman who does not notify the police will be assaulted again within the next six months: two in five.

The Harper's Index

1994 VITAL STATISTICS (last available data)

Birth rate: 13.2 per thousand

Marriage rate: 5.5 per thousand

Divorce rate: 2.7 per thousand

Median family income: $48,091

Percent of families with low income: 13.5

Women's full-time earnings as percentage of men's: 69.8

Statistics Canada

Family Structure

Male lone parents: 2.3 percent

Common-law couples with children: 4.1 percent

Common-law couples without children: 5.8 percent

Female lone parents: 10.7 percent

Married couples without children: 29.3 percent

Married couples with children: 47.8 percent

Statistics Canada

If you are a woman, you can expect to spend 18 years of your life helping an aging parent and 17 years caring for children.

The Vanier Institute of the Family

On any given day, three out of four women prepare family meals, but only one out of three men [do so].

The Vanier Institute of the Family

There are no markers in reality. Reality is a continuum of growth and development. The family, however, is designed to create markers.

Dr. Elise Boulding

Women will spend more years alone with their spouses than in the company of children; the opposite of what most married women have experienced...perhaps for most of human history.

Jones, Marsden & Tepperman
Lives of Their Own

In 1991, most poor children lived in two-parent families. But two out of every three children in single-mother families lived below the poverty line.

Profiling Canada's Families
The Vanier Institute of the Family

Seven in ten families with spouses of working age had both spouses working in 1994, compared with only three in ten in 1967. The presence of two earners in the family increases the likelihood that both will accumulate retirement pension benefits, eventually leading to more families with two pensioners.

Perspectives on Labour and Income
Statistics Canada, Autumn 1996

The number of middle-income families, that is, families with a combined income between $30,000 and $60,000 a year, has been declining since 1980 when they accounted for 44.4 percent of all families. By 1990, they had dropped to 41.4 percent; by the end of 1993, middle-income families accounted for 40.7 percent of all families – a 3.7 percent drop in 12 years. For every 12 middle-class families in 1980 there are now 11.

Daphne Bramhan and Gordon Hamilton
"The Death of the Middle Class"
Transition, *March, 1993*

Fewer and fewer men are doing the grocery shopping – just 15 percent now, according to a new survey conducted by the Food and Consumer Products Manufacturers of Canada and reported in *The Globe and Mail* in October, 1996. This is down from 1991 when 21 percent of the principal shoppers in Canada were men.

The Globe and Mail

From 1980 to 1994, an average of 11 percent of two-parent families had incomes below the Low Income Cut-Off (LICO); without transfer payments this would have been 17 percent. For lone-parent families, an average 54 percent had incomes below the LICOs (62 percent if no transfers).

Perspectives on Labour and Income
Statistics Canada, Autumn, 1996

PART ONE

WHAT IS A FAMILY?

1

Families in History

*He that would know what shall be, must consider what
hath been.*
– H.G. Bohn
Handbook of Proverbs, 1855

Like the farmer's legendary axe with three new heads and two new handles, the family has changed a lot over the years. But it still is the basic human institution. Change is implicit in life, of course; without it there is no growth, without it there is, in fact, no life. The family is definitely not dead. We can't afford to listen to anyone who says that it's dead and dying and beyond help. It's just changing again, as it must, as we must. Such changes dictate new definitions. Definitions follow after patterns, they don't cause them. The trick is to read the patterns.

By this time we think we know all about the descent of humanity from the apes: Darwin and all that, Desmond Morris's *Naked Ape*, Helen Fisher's *Sex Contract* (whereby the female is supposed to have stepped up her sex appeal in order to attract and persuade the male to protect her and the kids she was so busy bearing and feeding, thus, incidentally, creating a family). In any case, Elaine Morgan (*The Descent of Woman*) has a better idea of evolution, involving women, explaining some of the conundrums of evolution that the male viewpoint hasn't solved, and dating the nuclear family from cave days. Most anthropologists without an axe to grind agree that the family is hundreds of thousands of years old.

Those first families were groups – tribes or clans. As in later communities, the infant -bearing, -feeding, -grooming, food-foraging-mother was responsible for the young. Living arrangements defined these creatures as interdependent. Huddled on one shore or (inland) in one cave around several fires, under one longhouse roof, in one courtyard, in one large house, whatever was available over the centuries, people lived together in large familial groups.

When they settled down to herd or to farm, the herdsmen learned by watching their sheep what was causing all those babies in human females. This discovery reduced the awe in which women had been held. Men usurped life-and-death power over the females and the young, so that life for little ones, precarious at best, remained cheap and short. Infanticide, particularly female infanticide, was practiced for centuries, from classical Greek and Roman times, through the Middle Ages, right up to today; only the methods and timing (pre- or post-natal) differ. Babies had tough lives, that is if they survived being born, and often short ones, decreed less by God than by *man*. Of what importance was progeny, as such, when there were always more babies where those came from?

We are aware that present social doomsayers are crying that childhood is dead, that terrible things are happening to children today, that people don't revere children the way they used to, and also that children aren't acting like children anymore, that families are so fragmented and confused that they are on their way to becoming extinct. Ignoring infant (and maternal) mortality rates of centuries past, turning a blind eye to the child abuse and kiddie porn of "the other" Victorians, a deaf ear to the cries of starving infants dependent on a wet-nurse's not-so-tender mercies and of four-year-old chimney sweeps and nine-year-old miners, and waving a bland statistic at any other odious comparisons, they stoutly maintain their nostalgic belief in the superiority of the old ways and the 24-carat solidity of golden days.

Philippe Ariès, in his book *Centuries of Childhood*, claims that the concept of the family only emerged in the 16th and 17th centuries and that it is inseparable from the concept of childhood. Before then, a large household might comprise a number of disparate people with little distinction drawn between the servants, retainers and hangers-on, and the children of the house/manor/castle. In fact, the male children were often visiting, assigned by their aristocratic fathers to serve another lord and learn the ways of the world while the lower classes apprenticed their sons to a trade. Girls, of course, stayed home and learned to sew (but not to read) and to run the household.

Households were larger, obviously, and the home was a kind of factory with many workers/servants and one manager (usually the woman, the chatelaine), producing not only its own food but its own goods and services. When the man took command in the house, the woman became one of the servants; the servants retired to their own space; children became part of a smaller cohesive group related, usually, by blood, and the family as we recognize it started up.

With the advent of the Industrial Revolution productivity moved out of the home, along with the man, who left to work, leaving the woman at home to run things in the domestic sphere. By the 19th century, children became the chief focus and the career of women – upper-class women, of course, wives of men of means who could say proudly, "No wife of mine will ever work."

The Victorian family had an enormous effect on Western thinking, carrying over to the New World its sentimental treatment of children and its reverence for women, as long as there were lower-class sources of both for exploitation.

This capsule history of the family brings us to the latter half of the 20th century when the working wage has ceased to support a breadwinner's family; when married women, in unprecedented numbers, even those with children, have began to work outside the home for money to help hold it together; and when children now carry a price tag: $150,000 at last count to bring a no-frills child to the age of 18 when more money and attention must be paid. Marriage, the glue that shaped and held the family together, while still the pattern of choice, has become altered and eroded and reconstituted to the point of no return, at least, not with any guarantee of a refund.

The combination of fewer children (the Baby Boom was a glitch in history), divorce and remarriage, along with longer-lived grandparents, has resulted in the strange anomaly of most young people now having more parents than siblings. Feminism has been blamed for an economic necessity – women working outside the home – but the combination of feminism, joint custody, job mobility (not necessarily upward) and make-shift solutions to problems that will not go away, has left the family, wherever and whatever it is, in a state of confusion. Do we still know what a family is? If so, where is it headed? And where do we go from here?

Backwards, for a moment, to complete definitions and lay a base for discussion. How do we know where we're going till we know where we are and how we got here? Which way is forward? Out? Up?

2

What Is a Family?

A family is a unit composed not only of children,
but of men, women, an occasional animal, and the
common cold.
– Ogden Nash

Statistics Canada's census definition of family is almost too simple: "A married couple with or without never-married children or a single lone parent living together with never-married children." (Immediately I want to ask, what about the ones, married or not, who come back?) Couples who have lived together for a year or more are considered married. So far, same-sex couples have been omitted but the courts are being challenged as I write because the benefits at stake are worth fighting for.

Stats Can also defines as an "economic family" people who are related by blood, marriage, or adoption and who share a dwelling. The Canadian government, when gathering information, uses the term *household* for people, not necessarily related by blood, adoption, or marriage, who share a dwelling. Maureen Baker, who edited the 1996 (third) edition of *Families: Changing Trends in Canada*, reports that Canadian advocacy groups are recommending that definitions of family should be extended to allow for "caring and enduring intimate relationships regardless of legal or blood ties." In other words, structure and legality are becoming less important to the definition of family than the functions it performs and the services it provides.

A History of Private Life (vol. V) quotes Georg Simmel's definition of family:

> *A form that comes into being in many different ways, in which individuals constitute a unity on the basis of certain interests and ideals, either temporary or permanent, conscious or unconscious, and within which those interests are realized.*

The beauty of this definition is that it disregards blood, adoption, and marriage. I want to hang onto that idea of unity, also of *realization*.

Here are some more definitions (with my comments and questions) from the *Gage Canadian Dictionary*.

- *A father, mother and their children.* Are the children the offspring of the original father and mother? Are the parents still married to each other? Or are they members of a reconstituted family: Father Blue, Mother Yellow, with Blue children, Yellow children, and Green children from the new union?

- *The children of a father and mother.* Where do these children live? With their single mother, single father, with their stepfather or stepmother, in foster home(s), or, as in some cases I have read of, with each other, bringing themselves up rather than be separated (the situation of a popular television show, Party of Five).

- *One's spouse and children.* These days one's spouse is not necessarily the parent of all one's children, or even some or one of them. Maybe the children are the spouse's children and not one's own. Introductions get more difficult all the time.

➤ *A group of related people living in the same house.* People who live in the same house are not always related by blood. They can be related by a common interest, as are college students who live together for economy's sake. They can be residents of a group home brought together for communal living while they learn life skills to prepare them to live on their own (ex-convicts or ex-mental patients, developmentally handicapped people, unwed mothers, battered wives and their children and so on). And now, overtly, same-sex couples live together, often with a child they are parenting. Whatever the reasons that have brought any of these people together, while they live in the same house they function as a family.

➤ *All of a person's relatives.* These are the strange people one sees at family reunions, weddings, but not Canadian Thanksgiving. (Only Americans treat their November holiday like a political convention.) Other special events include christenings, bar and bat mitzvahs, funerals, Yom Kippur, Hanukkah, Christmas, and so on, all devised with varying degrees of ceremony to celebrate family festivals, rituals, additions and departures. Some families are closer than others; some celebrate more than others.

➤ *A group of related people, a tribe.* Some people are related, for a time at least, by a common cause, ranging from a political interest to a shared concern, such as bereavement, divorce, illness, alcoholism, or specific professional interests. The idea of tribe was revived by other than native peoples in the 1960s, when the flower children banded together in communes (or families). Novelist Margaret Laurence identified the members of The Writers' Union of Canada as a tribe. Marshall McLuhan predicted that the media would bring all the people of the world back into a tribal situation in a "global village." It hasn't happened yet.

➤ *Any group of related or similar things.* This definition, of course, refers more to the flora and fauna of the world than to the people who constitute families. In *Slapstick*, Kurt Vonnegut used the idea to create artificial families: people were grouped together at random under categories of flora or fauna. Thus, all the Daffodils were arbitrarily related – and found they had a surprising amount in common! We all do.

These are all abstract concepts, having very little to do with Real Life as we know it in today's families. A dictionary doesn't deal with case histories and statistics and can't begin to tell us what Canadian families face as they try to cope day by day by day. The Vanier Institute of the Family (VIF) offers not one definition but variations on a theme, describing different kinds of families.

➤ "Nuclear" families composed of two parents and their one or more children, living together.

➤ "Extended" families composed of parents, children, aunts, uncles, grandparents and other blood relations living together, or not.

➤ "Blended" or "recombined" or "reconstituted" families composed of parents who have divorced their first spouses, remarried someone else and formed a new family that included children from one or both first marriages, and/or from the re-marriage.

➤ "Childless" families consisting of a couple.

➤ "Lone-parent" families composed of a parent, most often a mother, with a child or children.

➤ "Co-habiting couples" and "common-law marriages" – family arrangements that resemble other forms, but without legalized marriage.

➤ "Traditional" families – a confusing term that reflects the changing nature of Canadian families in that people tend to use it to refer to their own families, or to the family type that they have encountered most often.

And what about the statistics? Staggering, and illuminating.

➤ Double-income families. (By 1993, 78.6 percent of married women between the ages of 35 and 44 were working for pay.)

➤ Lone-parent families. (In 1991, over 80 percent of all single-parent families were headed by women, a figure that hadn't changed much since the 1960s.)

➤ Blended families. (By 1991, 32.3 percent of marriages had at least one partner who had been married before, and more spouses were bringing their children into the new family.)

➤ Extended families. (One big happy family under one roof is a myth. Big but not happy; the number of multi-family households is declining as more single people, including old ones, prefer to live alone.)

➤ Co-vivants. Common-law partnerships now comprise 12 percent of long-term relationships. (I hesitate to use the word permanent.) Very close friends. Same-sex liaisons, both gay and lesbian, figure more and more prominently in society today. Hard to count them until they're on the books for benefits, which would affect about 56 laws. A number of these couples, both male and female, are rearing children. Teachers can't be too careful what they say or do for Mother's Day or Father's Day.

➤ Co-ops and communal experiments. Group homes have already been mentioned. I know a number of struggling theater people (actors, writers, directors) and other young people just starting out in the big city, who share accommodation until they get a stake. During their time of cohabitation, they behave with each other like family, eating together and arguing about whose turn it is to take out the garbage or clean the toilet.

All of these patterns of living represent family life in some form today, and each of them presents its own problems. It might help to go back to the prototype before we go forward.

There are two kinds of family: the family of origin, that is, the one each of us was born in, and the family of procreation, that is, the one most people move into and create with children of their own. Most people have the first, having sprung from somewhere. Not everyone, obviously, produces the second. As we know, and will observe, the forms families take differ a great deal.

For discussion's sake, consider my family of origin – the classic nuclear family. My father knew best. My mother stayed at home. My brother's name wasn't Dick, it was Jack. He's four years older than I am, and Mother always told me he was smarter than I was, that I shouldn't be too smart, and I certainly shouldn't work so hard or else I'd never get married. What I wanted more than anything was to be normal, not to be teased for being fat and smart, and not to be different. (Girls who were different had a very hard time.) My father went away to war (World War II) while all my friends' fathers stayed home and made money and all my friends' mothers hoarded pineapple juice. My mother was a single parent for five years.

Of course, I'm a Grey Eminence now. It's possible my children will be more typical of my readers. The four of them are part of the Big Generation, the 60 million Boomers born between 1946 and 1962. Not as rooted as my parents, my husband and I left the city where we were born and bred and took our children to a smaller city in another province where we were all stranded when my husband died prematurely. The children and I eventually moved, almost separately (two of them were in university), to a larger city in our struggle to survive. I remained a single working parent and have not remarried.

My three children who have married have had five marriages so far. The two who divorced and remarried are split again and both have joint custody of their children. I have a total of seven grandchildren. My youngest son is developmentally handicapped and lives with a roommate in a subsidized apartment assisted by the resources of a community living program. Thus, with our individual histories and life events, we manage to represent a number of the forms that families take today.

When people leave their families of origin and marry and raise families of their own, they create new families of procreation, which are the families of origin for their children. They bring patterns and rituals, lifestyles, assumptions and memories from their families of origin to their new family of procreation. Some of these things are whimsical but reinforcing, some are vicious and ingrained, some are self-fulfilling prophecies.

We used to say to my daughter Liz, "You should be a lawyer, you're so nit-picking." She isn't, but she acted as her own counsel for her (first) divorce, and she reminded me then of what we used to say. Actually, she's precise, like my aunt Alma.

This is what psychiatrist R. D. Laing (1927–1989) means in his book *The Politics of the Family*, when he speaks of the scripts we play out and carry from our family of origin into our family of procreation, where it starts all over again. But it's not merely the tapes that run in our head, it's the images we carry. Laing describes the family "as a shared fantasy image," usually a "container of some kind *in* which all members of the family feel themselves to be and *for* which image all members of the family may feel each should sacrifice themselves. Since this fantasy exists only in so far as it is 'in' everyone who shares 'in' it, anyone who gives it up, shatters the 'family' in everyone else." Maybe it's simpler to think of family as a container, implying as it does the physical shelter that encompasses it. Easier to deal with a concrete dwelling place than with fantasies and prophecies.

Apart from the prophecies, what about others' expectations? The old tapes don't work any more. Some of the expectations of behavior and performance are simply obsolete and have no relevance to what young people are facing today. We can't preach 4th-century birth control or 19th-century morality to a hi-tech generation. Words like abstinence, frugality, prudence, and self-sacrifice smack of Victorian righteousness and become a mockery in light of the changing ecology, to say nothing of 20th-century ethics and fading Judeo-Christian beliefs. We have to find new definitions of old concepts, new guidelines and new ways to teach them. In the meantime, let's agree that family is, indeed, a container, a crucible tempering and molding us, for good or ill.

What is more important is what families *do*, what families are *for*. Here again the VIF provides some guidance. Families, according to the Institute, take responsibility for various combinations of some or all of the following (my comments in parenthesis).

➤ Physical maintenance and care of group members. (That means feeding, clothing, and nursing in sickness and in health.)

➤ Socialization of children. (Examples of socialization: "What's the magic word?" or "You are not going out of the house like that!")

➤ Social control of members. (Not only nice girls don't, but nice boys don't either. If you can't say anything nice, don't say nothin' at all, as Thumper's mother once said. The Golden Rule. Honesty is the best policy, and now – don't litter!)

➤ Production, consumption, distribution of goods and services. (The family is the most important economic unit in the country, which is why governments are not averse to divorce because it requires duplication of goods and services and the accompanying taxes.)

➤ Affective nurturance. (The most rewarding, most demanding task of all, also known as TLC. It should be genderless.)

In the following chapters (Part Two: The Family in Action), I will look at each of these areas in more detail. We want to figure out what families do, how they function, and how they affect the society we live in today. What's going to happen tomorrow?

PART TWO

THE FAMILY IN ACTION

3

Feeding the Hungry, Clothing the Naked, Nursing the Sick

I have found the best way to give advice to your children
is to find out what they want and then advise them to do it.
— Harry S. Truman

CHILD-REARING

The question most parents want to ask about their children is how? How do they give their kids a sense of personhood? How do they get the idea into them about being responsible for themselves and others? And what about morality, and will they be happy, and can they be friends?

All this eagerness and anxiety comes with an overload of guilt. "Dear God," prays every conscientious new mother, "help me to be a good mother," already worried that she won't be. I'm not sure what fathers pray. They're caught in the Iron-John bind these days, trying to be male but sensitive too. In any case, both parents hope their children will be better.

Better than what? What does better mean? Happier? Richer? More successful? More competent? Better adjusted? To what? I found out what I really wanted for my children when I had a damaged child. I wanted him to become an independent, functioning human being, and he is, with a lot of help from his community. That, basically, is what we all want for our children. Independent and functioning aren't too hard to define, but what do we mean by *human being*, and how does that happen, after they're born, that is? How does it happen?

Not all by itself, not in a vacuum. "I am a part of all that I have met," wrote Tennyson, not the least of which is what we encountered in our so-called formative years. (Whoever stops forming?) Truly, all experience is an arch through which human beings pass on their way to – humanity? – which not everyone achieves. The state of being human, yes; the fact of being *humane*, that takes effort and time, a lifetime.

R.D. Laing fell out of fashion before his death in 1989, but he said some things that remain worth considering. I've already mentioned his suggestion that we live our adult lives in a sort of posthypnotic trance left over from our childhood, obeying commands and suggestions that are difficult if not impossible to erase. It's still a valid idea; most people, in fact, never come out of the trance. If they do, it's quite painful. Laing's idea is that everyone in a family is given a scenario and assigned a role. The family as "container" holds us firmly as we play our roles, perhaps repeating patterns that have been established and repeated over generations, acting parts that we have never read or seen but that we somehow know how to play. This kind of indoctrination in a different context is called brainwashing. It goes on in every family.

You hear people saying, "He's careful, like his uncle Harry." Or, "That boy will never amount to anything, he's so lazy." Or, "Isn't she a little mother?" Or, "You're just like your crazy Aunt Suzy, taking in every stray that comes along." Who wrote those scripts?

The social scientist Erving Goffman (1922–1983) saw the interaction of family members as a performance and noted the casting: the scapegoat, the peacemaker, the wild one, the klutz, and so on. Once cast, the players are forced by expectation and treatment to play true to type. Perhaps it would help if parents were more aware of labels and assumptions so that they don't saddle their children with self-fulfilling prophecies. The kids have enough other patterns and problems to deal with as it is.

Besides those labels and prophecies, there are other scenarios: We see young women marrying their fathers in the strong older men they think will take care of them, and young men marrying their mothers in the uncritical women in whom they hope to find the nurturing they crave. A daughter becomes the son her father never had; a boy becomes the mama's boy his prematurely widowed mother leans on until he bends.

This is another aspect of what Laing means when he speaks of the scripts we play out and of the posthypnotic commands we obey for the rest of our lives. It's not such a new idea now. Eric Berne published *Games People Play* in 1964, and spawned an entire self-help movement as people methodically examined the roles and scripts they'd been handed and forced to enact. The best way to (begin to) rewrite the script, especially the ending, is to see the knots we've been tied or tied ourselves into. (*Knots* is one of Laing's books, still in print, a perennial seller since its publication in 1970.)

Parents today are more aware than those of my generation that dire prophecies are not only self-destructive but also bound to come true. Tell a child often enough that he's stupid or selfish or lazy and he'll believe it and act accordingly. We have called the family of origin a crucible. Laing says it's a slaughterhouse. Goffman says it's a Siberia. These days it seems more like a junk emporium.

In its early days, television was welcomed into the lives of young children as a godsend to mothers, an "electronic babysitter." Now along with its cousin monitor (of computer games) it has become a powerful shaper of thoughts and attitudes. Parents today are looking forward to the V-chip, to help them control the gratuitous violence pouring into the home daily (it's estimated that by the time a child reaches the age of 16, he has seen something like 18,000 deaths), as if violence were the only thing that needs to be controlled. Some parents make an effort to screen or limit their children's viewing but unless they simply refuse to own a TV (I personally know only one parent who has taken this stance), the odds are against them.

As in everything else, there are fashions in child-rearing. My mother's generation believed in bottle-feeding babies strictly by the clock; my generation of mothers believed in the best of all permissive worlds according to Dr. Spock, and few of us breast-fed our infants; my children's generation brings the New Father right into the delivery room, straps the Snuggli firmly onto his manly chest, nurses the baby until the maternity leave is over, and hopes to raise children with sweet reason.

Where once the experts told mothers to go ahead and make strict rules, they then went on to question the behavior of both mother and child and to put us in a double bind, which they proceeded to question some more. By the 1970s, recognizing women's lack of power (because they were struggling for some, along with equal pay), hence their ineffectiveness, the experts began to look around to see who was actually empowering the omnipotent child. So now they're into family therapy, looking at the triad, that is, dealing with mother-father-child within the family situation – with maybe an abusive grandfather or an alcoholic grandmother thrown in?

It can get depressing when it's not terrifying. If the way we think and behave and respond is simply the result of a specific situation and particular relationships, that is, out of our control, rather than the situation and relationships being the result of our behavior and beliefs, it means we can't change without motivating the people around us to change as well. It means we have to do more than merely remove the "Kick Me" sign. It means that no one does anything of one's own volition. We're all knee jerks, reacting to someone else's little hammer. It's downright humiliating, not to say dangerous, if the hammer is in the hands of the child, the omnipotent one.

I can remember going into absolute panic when I brought my first child home from the hospital, so afraid, not that I was going to drop her but that I was going to do something wrong and damage her psyche. (Of course, I did.) My father spotted my anxiety and guessed the cause. He said to me, "I don't hold my parents responsible for everything I've become. At some point in my life I took over and started making my own decisions. I'm as much to blame as they are." That was reassuring. (Now someone tell my daughter.)

What I discovered was that parents aren't the only ones with the power. A child can have enormous power. I was seldom aware of how my children were manipulating me and pushing my buttons, although I could easily see how my friends were putty in their kids' hands. A disturbed power relationship can upset the balance in any family and hurt everyone. I've seen a stepchild wreck a new marriage and a dying child destroy a hitherto stable one. Sometimes the balance shifts when a special child is born into it – handicapped or disfigured or in some way different. In a case like that, sometimes outside help is needed. Goffman, wrote an entire book about the effect (*Stigma: Notes on the Management of Spoiled Identity*).

Whether "normal" or not – whatever normal means – we're talking middle class and all the concomitant values. It helps any family to have rules and a routine that lets its members know what is expected of them. It's good for kids to have someone decide for them – up to a point. They get to that point and past it soon enough, and they usually make it very clear when – in no uncertain terms. Before it comes, it helps to lay down the rules. Later, as the rules are reassessed and renegotiated, some guidance may be offered and may or may not be accepted. Of course, certain areas of activity and behavior – those to do with the child's safety, health, responsibility and basic morality – are not negotiable. They must therefore never be allowed into the arena of discussion or even be thought to be open to negotiation.

Thus, bedtime for a young child is not negotiable, because a child needs a certain number of hours of sleep (some less than others, true). Good nutrition is essential for health and should not become a bone/candy of contention. Keeping promises – on both sides; doing what one says one is going to do – on both parts – these are not negotiable. Certain expectations and standards of behavior must be honored and it saves a lot of time for all concerned if there is no argument. Other duties such as homework and some home help may be more flexible but are still not negotiable. All members of the family have to contribute to the well-being and smooth-functioning of the organism, according to their abilities. Certain standards of morality, whether based on a religion or on society's laws and compassion's admonitions, may be the subject of an interesting discussion with an argumentative teenager, but with little leeway when it comes to behavior. Lies, theft, property damage and bodily harm remain unacceptable. "Rules is rules."

Children need limits. Setting limits actually frees them, gives them a feeling of security, helps them know how far they can push and what is the pale beyond which they must not venture. If they can't observe the limits, if they aren't ready to meet the restrictions or, conversely, to handle freedom, then stricter limits must be imposed. It will help them in later life to understand clearly that consequences follow the breaking of rules. It's a tough lesson to learn and one that not every adult fully understands or adheres to.

Children also need autonomy. If greater freedom is granted as children go along, feel ready and ask for it, then it is accompanied by a feeling of pride for having earned it and of self-respect for being deemed worthy of it. Most parents make the mistake of underestimating their children's maturity and skills and of trying to keep them young and under wraps for too long, particularly the eldest child.

"It isn't fair," she yells. "Not fair. I wasn't allowed to do that until I was ten!"

Whatever the privilege is, she can be told that she has led the way for her siblings. Besides, it's easier with two or three of them to go along with the one-rule-fits-all-sizes, not always fair, but easier.

Children need attention. The reason a lot of kids stop telling their parents anything is that a lot of parents don't pay attention to anything their kids are saying. It's amazing how many parents don't listen to their children. An absent-minded "that's nice, dear" won't do when the news is earthshaking to the child. And when kids have a grievance or a problem, something to negotiate, they require full attention and gravity. Listening should start at an early age so that the habit of communication is established – non-judgmental listening, no editorials. If the listener is seen as sympathetic and wise (I wish!), then perhaps at a later time some advice might be tolerated.

I can't stand this. I sound as if I know everything. I don't. It's just that I'm out of the crucible now and I can look back with detachment, cool and unpressured. I yelled at my kids. I was unfair, inconsistent, impatient and an adrenaline addict. Also tired, worried, harassed, overworked and isolated in a suburban bungalow with four children. The oldest one was in Grade One when the brain-damaged one was born. I don't yell anymore, not because I have improved, but because my children have. Also grown up and moved out. There's no one for me to yell at.

I remember a character called Agnes in a novel by Angela Thirkell. Agnes had more children than I did, but she also had excellent help. When one of her children fell into a puddle, Agnes admonished the child mildly: "Wicked one! Wicked one! Go see Nanny!" I was struck dumb with admiration for such forbearance. But then I didn't have a nanny. I was the nanny. If a kid of mine got muddy, I was the one who had to clean up the mess. So I said more than Agnes did, a lot more, quite loudly, and with some feeling. It seemed to give me energy as I cleaned up the mess.

It still comforts me to quote Pearl Buck: "Some are kissing mothers and some are scolding mothers, but it is love just the same, and most mothers kiss and scold together."

I notice my daughters are more patient than I was. I probably set them an effective negative example but I think that the fact that they work outside the home has more to do with it. They are not in the constant company of their little ones for 24 hours of each day. They get to talk to adults and to use different parts of their brains. I was one of the mothers of the Big Generation, a worker in the insane cohort that Betty Friedan released with her mind-blowing book, *The Feminine Mystique*. My oldest child was nine when the book was published and that's when she began making her own bed, leading the way for her siblings. Kids today start younger and do dishes too. Everyone has to pitch in.

This is because both their parents are working.

CHILDREN OF WORKING PARENTS

At work you think of the children you've left at home.
At home, you think of the work you've left unfinished.
Such a struggle is unleashed, your heart is rent.
– Golda Meir

Surely child-rearing, which includes all those directives (feeding the hungry, clothing the naked…), is difficult enough when it is one's sole job, with all its concomitant responsibilities. It becomes a monumental task if a parent (still usually female, but the patterns are slowly changing) adds to this the stress and time involved in holding down a job outside the home. On top of that *she* usually feels guilty because she's not doing enough and should be there. Where? Two places at once.

I've talked to enough working mothers to know how torn they feel about leaving their children in day care. No matter how carefully they have chosen the facility or the caretaker, they still feel it could be better or they should be there, and they keep wondering if they've made the right choice. After the child/children start school there's before and after to worry about, not to mention Professional Development Days. Then the parent fusses with stopgap solutions and after-school programs. After they have agonized over the solutions and the facilities, parents go back to agonizing over the choice. Given all the other choices made before this one, they have no choice.

Even as I write, governments – our practically peerless leaders – still don't seem to realize that the double-income family is a given these days and not likely to go away. They are attempting cuts and compromises on every level while the long-awaited promise of universal child care remains just that – a promise, unkept, unhonored, unrecognized in its importance. A current suggestion is to decrease the already low salary of day-care workers and increase the number of children in their care. As it is right now, garbage collectors make more than day-care workers, perhaps because society cares more about trash than it does about children? Certainly people are concerned about the future of landfill.

In the meantime, working families find different, seldom satisfactory and seldom permanent, means of taking care of their children while they work. Professional caregivers, low paid as they are, are beyond the means of most working parents, especially single mothers without subsidies, which are being/have been cut. Some nursery schools and child-care centers subsidize themselves with co-op efforts supplied by the parents. Pre-kindergarten is also being/has been cut by squeezed and decreased education grants. Some new mothers opt for stay-at-home bonding and take in one or two (no more than three) paying guests – babies or pre-schoolers – to care for since they're at home anyway. Other mothers use in-home caregivers, be they members of the family, live-in or -out help – au pair girls, daytime housekeepers, visiting or full-time nannies, and so on – all paid, of course, and rigid about schedules. ("Be home on time, or else I quit!")

Since child care is substitute mothering, or supposed to be, parents try to choose as carefully as they can, but frequently their backs are to the wall. Ideally, the prospective caregivers should be carefully interviewed and the operation and facilities of the child-care center inspected (some centers require it of the parents). The child, of course, should be helped to adjust to the arrangement, and to the separation from the parent, not just dumped. Ideally, too, the caregiver should be screened for age, cleanliness, stamina (a must!), speech (grammatical), language (free of profanity), gender attitudes, training and experience. Most ideally of all, the caregiver should love children. Or else find another job.

The ratio of caregivers to children is important, too, and about to be decreased, if the current attrition of day care continues. The younger the child the more caregivers there should be, not only for cuddling and care and stimulation, but also to avoid being parked in a crib all day, left to fester in a dirty diaper.

Private enterprise has been providing some employees with day care, recognizing it sooner than governments for the necessity it is. Surely it is not the role of individual businesses to care for the nation's children, nor can they ever possibly offer universal care as government must. Here and there, unions have been pressuring management to establish workplace care facilities. Some companies offer a choice of benefits now: day care or a dental plan, for example. As always, the options present difficult choices to parents. In the case of two working parents, they can choose different benefits and supplement each other's perks.

No matter what kind of arrangements have been set up for the child, they all disintegrate when the kid gets sick. At first this happens quite often, because of the increased exposure to so many alien germs. One of the biggest open secrets of nursery-level day care is the rampant spread of gastro-enteritis among babies. A family physician told me there are cases of babies in day care contracting lifelong giardiasis (a mean, contagious form of intestinal anarchy). Apart from that chilling prospect, the children do develop an immunity; they have to sooner or later. In any case, the parents must have alternate plans for days when the child is too sick to go out or to be welcomed among the well ones. This again involves a few hard decisions before the fact.

Usually the parent earning the lowest income stays home with the sick child, because the economic risk in case of job loss is lower. (The question is, of course, what does a single parent do?) Fathers admit that they suffer a certain loss of face if they are the ones on call. Care of a sick child is still considered women's work. Many employee interviews require women to reveal their child-care arrangements, while rarely questioning the men. It is still assumed that somewhere, somehow, a woman is taking care of all that. Employers also assume, as American feminist writer Letty Cottin Pogrebin comments, "that workers will rob their personal lives to pay for their economic survival rather than upset traditional male-female power relations." In other words, child care is still considered the responsibility of the mother.

More and more parents are choosing not to destroy their personal lives. The idea of sacrificing their children to their jobs is increasingly repugnant. As employers begin (slowly) to realize this change in attitude, perhaps workplace day-care provision will be more readily available. Most parents haven't yet dug in their heels and rebelled in enough numbers to make their priorities clear. Soon. Maybe. Every family considers its own case so individual and personal that every time they hit a crisis parents think they're making a unique, one-time choice. They keep on juggling their own lives and the lives of their children without realizing that others are doing the same thing. Again, it's a matter of getting the priorities straight, and then of realizing that there is bargaining strength in numbers.

One of the fears of workplace day care is that the employee will become too dependent on it and be unable to leave the job for the sake of the child's continuity. How long does this bind last? School takes over from day care sooner or later, so the placement isn't forever. Then there is a small wave of young mothers trying to stay at home at least for those tender early years, taking a short sabbatical from their work, if they can afford to. Not many can, though, and not the ones who need day care the most.

It would behoove both the governments and the private sector to make day care available, feasible and affordable. The myth of the nuclear family persists longest in the minds of the politicians. They seem to think that the present state of affairs – with over three-quarters of married women in the work force, including mothers of pre-school children, and with the number growing all the time, out of necessity – is just a glitch in time. One morning they will wake up and find all the women back in their kitchens, barefoot and pregnant and providing "free" care for the nation's children. It has been several decades now since one bread-winner's salary was sufficient to support a spouse and family. The double-income family is here to stay. That being the case, day care is a national necessity.

Employers, too, those who want undivided loyalty from their employees, or at least some gratitude, are going to have to provide safe, adequate, convenient, affordable workplace day care. They have to realize that while it is possible to take the day care out of the mother it is impossible to take the mothering out of day care.

Some families, if they can afford it, prefer a live-in or at least an in-home nanny. My daughter in Boston was able to buy this kind of help when her children were tiny because the city is home to a large immigrant Irish population. My granddaughters were more in danger of developing an Irish accent than a Boston one!

What everyone thinks they want, of course, is a Mary Poppins, but she was a very versatile nanny. Before parents decide to look for such a paragon, that is, if they're lucky enough to be able to choose their options, they should consider what is most important to them. Some mothers want security and routine for their children; others want good English and decent manners; others are sticklers for cleanliness, regular fresh air and good nutrition. One cannot have everything. It must be remembered, too, that only a certain amount of loyalty can be bought; it must be earned by being a fair employer. As for friendship, that is an unsolicited gift. Nannies are more apt to fall in love with their small charges than with their employers.

School age children cost less to care for during the school year with so much of their time taken up, but they still have to be occupied and cared for during the summer. Community day camps abound, with different emphases on sports and crafts and creation. Boarding camps, while expensive, are also popular. Most families wait and take their vacations together. Probably there is more variety in summer activities and solutions than during the school year. The lower the family income, the fewer options there are.

I spoke to one young woman with one child, a nine-year-old boy who hadn't seen his father for three years. She hadn't seen a support payment for the same length of time and she couldn't afford to collect; her ex was 3,000 miles away. Even with the so-called government help now, the lines are busy and it takes a lot of precious time to get through. Anyway, Darline, as I'll call her, had a respectable but low-paying job. She said that during the school year she managed to scrape together a little money, to try to get ahead, but that every summer her nest egg was wiped out because she had to pay for some kind of summer camp and child care to keep her son off the streets while she worked.

I met another young women, a divorced mother of two, who had been making good money as a life insurance agent, but who returned to her profession, nursing, because she could work nights and be home for her children during the day. I asked her if she slept. "Not much," was the reply. Less fortunate women, that is, earning less money than a nurse, work as night cleaners for the same reason – to be there for the kids.

After an abstract consideration of child-rearing and a recognition of the hopes and fears all parents harbor about the future of their children, it's a bit daunting to realize how swiftly long-term goals disappear in the actual daily activity of just doing it.

A day in the life of an intact double-income family involves pressure, planning and timing just to get the principals in their places each morning. Enough energy is expended to power General Motors and the day hasn't started. At the other end, when everyone is gathered again, other pressures build: homework, laundry (some things can't wait until the weekend), the cooking and cleanup of the evening meal, preparation for the next day, some effort at communication and relaxation, that is, when there aren't sports or choir practices to rush off to, or lessons or rehearsals, club or school meetings, volunteer coaching or guiding, and so on and so on.

Weekends rush by, crammed with errands and shopping for groceries and services, cleaning, laundry, kids' activities, sometimes church, sometimes visits with family and friends, sometimes even a little rest. The good news is that most families spend their weekends together. Separated during the work week, they are seldom apart over Saturday and Sunday. When parents are home, they're really home. They rarely go out as a couple, choosing instead to spend their time with other families, en masse. They read to their children, rent movies to watch at home with them, do their chores around and with them, and take them on their errands and trips.

Talk about quality time! It looks pretty quantitative, too. That's in the early years, of course. Later, when the children get older, running the family becomes more a question of traffic control than of supervision, and the fridge door becomes information headquarters.

All this activity has caused a revolution in the marketplace, quicker to respond than government. Take-out and fast-food outlets have turned eating into family entertainment, with clowns and games and giveaways. Speed and simplicity guarantee that even a very small child will eat something before boredom and restlessness set in. The menus may be limited and not entirely healthful but the food purveyors at least know who their customers are: the whole family, all together.

In the 1950s, I think it was McCall's magazine that launched the togetherness theme. It was an idea whose time had come: the family that plays together stays together, and all that rather maudlin sentiment that went hand in oven mitt with somethin' lovin' cookin' in the oven. Elaine Taylor May (*A History of Private Life*) comments on this era that I lived through.

> *What is most remarkable about the family ideology after WWII is the polarized gender roles that it contained. In spite of the new emphasis on togetherness and companionate marriage, the distinct roles for male breadwinners and female homemakers reflected a separation of the sexes more reminiscent of the Victorian era than anything in the twentieth century.*

It's possible those years reproduced the Victorian family with greater fidelity and more sentiment than it had enjoyed the first time round. As one of the parents responsible for the Big Generation, I must say that we practiced a lot of togetherness but in many ways it wasn't as genuine as the togetherness of today's families. This may seem surprising at a time when even very young children are sent out to be cared for and picked up at the end of each day in accordance with their parents' working hours.

Older kids develop a different routine. They quickly learn to check that fridge door bulletin board for instructions. Because school hours don't match work hours many children, aged 11 or 12, at which they can be legally left alone for a short time, must fend for themselves. And so we have what are known as latchkey children.

A 1988 survey cited in the June, 1995, issue of *Transition* (the magazine about families, for families, published by the Vanier Institute of the Family) reported that 21 percent of Canadian children between the ages of six and 12 were latchkey. Just as the number of mothers working outside the home has increased, so this number will also have increased. Latchkey kids let themselves into the house and take care of themselves until the parents or parent gets home – they're either in double-income families or lone-parent families. They know the house rules, about not opening the door to strangers, and not giving away their parents' absence on the phone. I used to have a signal for my kids when I wanted them to answer; I am told parents still do this, or use a Vista phone.

After I was widowed, my youngest child would have become a latchkey child when I had assignments that kept me away during the day. However, I signed him up for after-school courses, programs run by volunteers (that is, other parents) from the Home and School Association. The kids learned cooking, dramatics, macramé, floor hockey and so on. The real purpose of this extracurricular education was to keep them occupied and off the streets until closer to the time when their parents came home from work. At the inner-city school my son attended, children of lone-parents or double-income parents were given priority.

I have spoken to teachers at schools across the country where, not by legislation but out of kindness and concern, a teacher will come early each day and open the school so that there is a safe warm place for children whose parent(s) must leave home before they do. I also know teachers in inner-city schools who keep a box of cereal in their desk drawer for kids who haven't had breakfast, and I met one principal who had a couple of extra cots put into the First Aid room so that children who needed sleep more than a spelling lesson might get some rest. Unsung social workers, all, and what's to become of their young charges with tighter budgets and work-to-rule?

And then we have Block Parents, a continent-wide phenomenon whose major catalyst was probably the anxiety of working mothers. Block Parents, as we all know by now, are people at home who display a sign in their window to indicate their willingness to help a child in distress. The sign tells a child that someone trustworthy is available in case of an emergency. Along with that back-up provision, parents try to teach their children "street smarts," the built-in caution that helps to protect them from strangers asking for directions or offering a lift or candy.

Knowing what to do and where help is available and how to get it is a necessary skill even for very young children these days. I know single mothers who teach their children their full names and phone numbers and how to dial the emergency number before they teach them nursery rhymes. It's a survival skill, just as watching out for saber-toothed tigers must have been in eons past. Older children can be put through fire drills or other emergency training ("What would you do if...?"), and tested for their knowledge of exits, location and use of the fire extinguisher if they're old enough to handle it, in addition to some other useful phone numbers.

The working child, that is, the child of working parents, develops other skills before long. As the kid gets older and more competent (not necessarily more mature), Mother starts phoning about 4:30 every afternoon to issue instructions about dinner. "You'll find a casserole on the third shelf of the fridge. Take it out and turn the oven on to 350° (she still tends to use Fahrenheit). When the light goes out, put the casserole in the oven. You might tear up some lettuce for a salad, if you feel like it."

Working single mothers save all their housework until Sunday afternoon (I did). They throw the laundry in (timed right in an apartment building, it's possible to do four or five wash loads at once); one of the kids vacuums, another dusts, the little one (that many kids?) empties the wastebaskets. Surveys have indicated that a single parent with three children actually spends ten hours less a week on housework than a married woman with a husband and two children. Interesting.

Ideally, when both parents work, the chores are supposed to become a family affair. An early survey revealed that when the wife went to work full time, thereby doubling her working hours, the husband increased his share of housework by up to nine minutes a day. Newer reports bring him up to an extra four hours a week! Children, however, can be remarkably helpful, although they still don't hang up their wet towels or put their clothes any-where but on the floor.

There are other working children – older kids who have part-time jobs. I am tempted to say that such employment is more common among chil-dren of single parents, but I know this is not necessarily so. Some families manage to get along only by dint of every able-bodied person in the house-hold working.

A working student is still a minor and needs help to keep in balance. There is still the major commitment to education that must be honored. A job must not be permitted to interfere too drastically with study time, sleep-ing time, and other necessities. At the same time, the responsibility to the employer must be met. It's a question of balance, something everyone has to learn sooner or later in order to stay cool.

STRESS

Stress: 1. constraining force; physical, mental, or emotional pressure or strain; stresses of urban living. 2. a state or condition resulting from such pressure or strain; suffering from stress.
– Gage Canadian Dictionary

I am not for a minute suggesting that women stop running in the fast lane and go back to the kitchen track. Staying home should be a positive choice, not a negative solution. Stress is not a male prerogative, as women in the working world are now proving. Women's smoking has increased, more than men's, and so have cigarette- and stress- related diseases among women. There has to be a connection.

Anyway, in my day women at home weren't stressed. Their doctors told them so. They were "restless"; they were "dissatisfied"; they didn't know a good thing when they had it – so they were told. (They were suffering from what Betty Friedan called "the problem with no name.") They were prescribed Valium so they would be grateful. Stress – *real* stress – belonged to men and the world of business. Not anymore. Now with women working full time as well as running the house and caring for the family in the 40 or 50 hours of spare time they give to that, they're entitled to some stress of their own. And they're getting it.

The career woman has her pressures. She is learning that she must seek help for the stress she feels, or else stop trying to be all things to all people. Like most upper-middle-class achievers, she is addicted to perfection. Women's magazines recognize her plight with humor, at the same time jumping at the chance of a great photo shoot: describing her esoteric dinner parties (breast of squid on a mango leaf, with a sauce made of sundried raspberries, and for dessert a white chocolate reproduction of Picasso's *Guernica*); her achieving child (creating his own computer programs at age three); her prowess in her field (brain surgery on Siamese twins joined at the head, or mistress-minding a billion-dollar merger between two yogurt giants); her easy good looks, skin, hair, clothes; her divinely handsome, rich husband who wouldn't dream of looking at another woman (but who, when he does, falls for a seeming airhead who pampers him with meat loaf and homemade peanut butter cookies).

Since the 1980s, women have been dazzling us with their balancing act, making life on the high wire look easy, making the rest of us feel like guilty failures. "Having it all" has become not just a way of life but a religion and most women's mags still taunt us with impossible role models along with advice on diet and exercise plus delicious desserts; cosmetics and clothes plus cookies; sexual behavior in the bedroom and the boardroom. Men's magazines, on the other hand, are still into the perfect Bloody Mary (the secret is horseradish), the perfect fly (for fishing), and Calvin Klein look-alike clothes. This is not to say that men are not under stress, too. They are. In his book *The Sibling Society*, American writer Robert Bly, who began as a poet and made a big name as the Iron Man, advises men to grow up and recover their macho self-esteem. Women must learn to accept men's differences. (So many responses spring to mind that I shall remain wordless.)

As a way of life, having it all has begun to pall. Women, at least, in the 1990s are being more realistic (or maybe cynical) about the amount of help they're going to get. A 16th-century English aphorism described a woman as "a shrew in the kitchen, a saint in the church, an angel at the board, and an ape in the bed." By the 19th century she had become the Angel of the House, revered by Henry James, later mocked by Virginia Woolf, who described her as the one willing to sit in a draft and take the leg of the chicken. Not much has changed. She's added the role of Ms. Efficiency in the office as she rushes home to do the shopping, the cooking and the cleaning and give quality time to the children and TLC to her husband to keep the marriage "alive." No wonder she's almost dead. Is this stress or burn out?

Oddly enough, though she may be tired, this Superwoman of the '90s is remarkably well. Surveys indicate that she is happier and less "restless" than her counterpart in the 1950s and 1960s. Her changing role(s) have given her a challenge and she has risen to it. Perhaps in response to that, we have The New Man – actually, he's been around for at least a decade – who is an Iron Man for the '90s. He has entered the labor room with enthusiasm (a bit daunted by all the blood, I am told), and can give a good back rub, carry a child (on his back or shoulders), cook up a mean stir-fry and help with the shopping.

The key word is *help*. He still expects his wife to make the plans and the shopping list, and he'll follow her lead. Note that while men's attitudes have changed – an increasing percentage say they think husbands of working wives should help with the housework – their behavior still hasn't caught up with their beliefs. Most of them still don't share the home work equally unless they have joint custody.

The patterns shift during and after a divorce; not only the amount of work but also the amount of money changes the status quo. Studies reveal that a wife's power in the decisions over money increases with every thousand dollars of income she brings into the house. So, too, do the odds of divorce. Yet another study reports that a man can be jealous of his wife's work, particularly if she makes more money than he does; fortunately for him, this doesn't happen very often. He likes the money his wife brings in, but he also likes to have her there when he needs her, ready and waiting and welcoming and attentive and nurturing, because it's a jungle out there and he doesn't want to hear about her jungle. Actually, it's the women who leave once they have some discretionary money. In those cases, it's not the jungle they mind so much as the animal at home.

If a man feels threatened by his wife's success, he should ask himself why, instead of dumping guilt on her, or making impossible demands, or accusing her of being "less than a woman," or denying sex (men do it too in more subtle ways than headaches). Marriage is not a competition. Marriage should be the source of ease, not stress. We can get stress anywhere.

Sociologist Jessie Bernard published her landmark book *The Future of Marriage*, in 1972, but she is still quoted and still valid in her famous claim that in every marriage there are two marriages: his and hers. His is happier than hers is. Hers is more stressful because what she needs is a wife.

Everyone knows what a wife is supposed to do; it's part of the basic training that has been going on in families since Victorian times. She has to be the Angel of the House. This socially indoctrinated concept haunts every working mother – the Ghost of Mothers Past – and guarantees a heavy load of guilt. (American writer Erica Jong said you don't have to beat a woman if you can make her feel guilty.) Guilty Mom thinks she's damaging her children, denying them the right to full-time mothering. It certainly was part of the 1950s ideology, the one I cut my children's teeth on. We had our demands of perfection laid on us, too, but very few, if any, of us gave our children our undivided attention, even though we were home with them. Quality time, as it is called, is quality time. A really good day care would ease most young mothers' guilt, and a strapping, faithful cleaning woman would take care of the rest.

Family stress is different from busy-ness because it has to be dealt with, not merely eased or covered over. Most families can't avoid stress by one or the other or both of the parents quitting or taking a less demanding, lower-status job. (There is no lower-status job than a parent's!) Family stress indicates more than burn out or tiredness; it means cracks in the foundation. The symptoms can't be treated without dealing with the cause, changing the system – easier said than done. Parents can't change jobs or quit, though some of them try. They have to pay attention to the warning signals, that is, if they want to stay married and hang on to their kids. Busy as they are, parents have to pay attention to the noises, the hurting sounds, the (sometimes muffled) cries for help.

Before the trouble is too severe for anything but professional therapy, parents can be alert to warning signs of stress in their children.

➤ Good behavior. This can happen after a divorce or a death in the family or some such major emotional event. A child will become the helpmate, the strong, reliable comforter of the afflicted parent, terribly responsible, sensitive – in short, too well behaved. I have met a number of young people like this, in the psychiatric units of hospitals. The unnaturally good behavior is the child's effort to regain the parent's attention, to be "loved best," to be reassured that he or she is still valuable within the family.

➤ Acting out, rebelliousness. This is perhaps a more common method of attracting attention. It's another bid for help. Boys particularly, so I have observed, go this route. The devil-may-care attitude is an attempt to show that nothing bothers the kid, but it's also a plea to be listened to.

➤ Increased aggression. We all get angry when life deals us a staggering blow. Anger is a legitimate part of the grief process and necessary to ultimate recovery. Anger often gives us the energy we need to go on, if we focus it right. But if it takes the form of antisocial aggression, it has to be re-channeled. Unhealthy aggression can be recognized in several familiar forms:

   ➤ fights with siblings;

   ➤ arguments, about everything;

   ➤ absenteeism, from home, from school;

   ➤ late arrivals, for dinner, for family engagements, or even no-shows.

These are not just bids for attention but also attempts to control an environment that has become too alien and too uncaring.

➤ Whining. A younger child who hasn't the means to make a statement by overt physical acts can resort to whining and clinging to the remaining parent. When the bottom has dropped out of a child's life as he or she knows it, a desperate clutching at straws is a natural reaction.

➤ Poor appetite, too, can be a form of protest and not only a response to a stomach that is sending out distress signals. Such stress behavior in (usually female) teenagers is recognized now as anorexia nervosa, or its converse, bulimia. It can indicate a desperate refusal to allow the body to mature, a terrible need for recognition by manipulating one's self-image, a frequently fatal method of commanding parents' attention or love.

➤ Poor sleeping habits. No adult sleeps well when worried about something. Neither do kids. Warm milk and night-lights were invented for people, young and old, with sleeping disorders. Again, as with every other stress symptom, attention must be paid – to the source and the cause.

It just may be that the children are trying to tell us something.

Male stress is something else again, although, as I say, women may be catching up in this department. They've still a way to go. Men are still the chief victims of stress-related heart attacks and strokes, and men still have a much higher suicide rate than women. (More women attempt it but more men succeed.)

For all I seem to be so annoyed with men, it's nice to have them around, preferably healthy and preferably home. I'm sure that some of the mid-life dumps that men perpetrate on their first wives are caused by stress. When they opt for a different, younger model and a different lifestyle, they're actually trying to find R&R as well as their vanished youth. For the sake of keeping both spouses healthy and emotionally balanced and for the sake of keeping them, period, it might be useful to consider a few warning signs of marital stress – husbands first.

- ➤ Husband makes critical comments in private on wife's cooking/ looks/children/housekeeping/intelligence.
- ➤ Husband makes critical comments in public on wife's cooking/ looks/children/housekeeping/intelligence.
- ➤ Husband is jealous of men in her life.
- ➤ Husband flirts with other women (or men? – sometimes gay men come out of the closet after years of marriage).
- ➤ Husband has extramarital affair(s) – if "accidentally" discovered, it's really bad news.
- ➤ Husband is silent, uncommunicative, uncooperative.

What is really at stake are the causes of marital stress. These symptoms are messages from the male side to the female; let it not be assumed that wives are incapable of dealing out similar messages. Here's how they do it.

- ➤ Wife makes critical comments (publicly and/or privately) on her husband's lack of sexual prowess/career failure/financial weaknesses/wimpy behavior.
- ➤ Wife overspends, running into debt on the charge cards.
- ➤ Wife has headaches, that is, denies sex, or shuts her eyes and thinks of Queen Victoria. (Some husbands have been known to develop necrophilia, proving that one can get used to anything.)
- ➤ Wife accuses her husband of never listening and then...
- ➤ She never listens.
- ➤ Wife indulges in conspicuous flirtation with other men.
- ➤ Wife drinks too much.
- ➤ Wife has an affair and, more important, lets it be discovered.

These may all be symptoms. What about the causes?

Russian novelist Leo Tolstoy said that happy families are all alike, that only unhappy families differ from each other. Not that he was a great family man himself, but in agreeing with Tolstoy I'll sidestep the specifics of unhappiness and try simply to identify the major issues that damage or break up marriages and families. I read the title of a new book on the subject, something about the seven causes of marriage breakdown. I didn't read the book, but I made my own list of the Big Seven:

> ➤ money
> ➤ sex
> ➤ children
> ➤ in-laws
> ➤ infidelity (different from adultery)*
> ➤ lack of communication
> ➤ lack of trust.

Different people might come up with a few different issues that cause a breakup. It's an interesting discussion, but it's not a parlor game and there are no winners. I see I didn't mention love. That, of course, is what it's all about. I think the best way to deal with marital stress is the way to deal with stress in children: with attention, patience, praise, sincerity, communication, respect, affection and time. Time is what every family needs, love enough and time.

Maybe it was easier when they had the church to help. A lot of parents these days figure they can teach their children morals without cluttering them up with religion. (For religion in this context read "bias.") The word religion, by the way, comes from the Latin *religio*, meaning "respect for what is sacred, probably originally, care (for worship and traditions)" (*Gage Canadian Dictionary*).

---

* There are many more ways of being unfaithful than merely with the body. Alcoholics are unfaithful; so are people who devote themselves to less lethal pastimes such as golf or business. What is commitment but loyalty?

This next little item may have nothing to do with what our children learn, but another survey has indicated that more marriages last and last longer among regular churchgoers. Do we attribute this phenomenon to tradition or habit or conformity? To paraphrase an old saying, does the family that prays together stay together?

Never underestimate the power of prayer. It doesn't matter what denomination or language the prayer is in, or even whether it's out loud, it is, as they say, the thought that counts. The important thing is the attempt to formulate one's thoughts and to communicate them. If the family is indeed fortunate enough to have a positive belief system, it's easier, that's all, but even without it, prayer/communication is still possible. It certainly isn't necessary to refer to God anthropomorphically.

"If I need to name God, it is better for me to say simply 'God,'" writes British theist Daphne Hampson, while agreeing with Alice Walker (*The Color Purple*) that "trying to do without him is a strain."

Walker's character Shug tells Celie, "You come into the world with God. But only them that search for it inside find it."

And it doesn't matter what we call God: him, her, or it. God within, God without. Getting in touch with one's innermost feelings, gaining some insight into one's self, actually attempting to communicate some idea of one's problems, one's care, in private – that's what prayer is. Like chicken soup, it doesn't hurt and it might help.

4

One Plus One Equals More

Television is the new member of the family.
It has replaced grandmothers and uncles
of the extended family and given Mother –
who inherited single-handedly all the housekeeping chores
the extended family once did cooperatively – some peace
and quiet.
– Jane O'Reilly

Among that list of tasks described by the Vanier Institute, one of the most important is the absorption of new members through procreation or adoption. As usual, no one has ever said this was easy. Depending on the point of view, that is, the parent's, the sibling's, or the new member's, there's a different story for each one.

SIBLING RIVALRY

My brother was an only child.
– Jack Douglas

Even people who never cracked a psychology book know the term *sibling* and the phrase *sibling rivalry*. Magazine and armchair psychologists never run out of wise things to say about siblings: the achieving first-born, the quiet middle one, the scrappy youngest. It's watered-down Adler (one of Freud's early bright disciples) and we still live by the stereotypes. We think we know all about the Battering Ram Eldest, the Neglected Middle, the Wait-For-Me Baby, the Prodigal Son, the Scapegoat, the Nosy One, the Tattletale, and so on. It's not just pop psychology, not anymore. A book by American social historian Frank Sulloway, published in October, 1996, has come up with a Darwinian view of human behavior that discounts such Freudian theories as the Oedipus complex. In *Born to Rebel*, Sulloway cites sibling rivalry as the "engine of history," backing up his claims with a massive amount of statistical evidence to prove the importance of birth order. First-borns are more conservative, later-borns more freethinking, and rarely do they see eye to eye.

I've already mentioned the dangers of typecasting and self-fulfilling prophecies. We all send messages, especially subliminal ones, especially in families. Not all of them are harmful, of course. Where but in the bosom of one's family can one learn moral outrage, the rankling sense of injustice when one's siblings are treated (*perceived* as being treated) better than one-self? Where can one learn the art of civil disobedience with such impunity, and the skill of negotiation, both verbal and physical? Where else can one learn so early and so well that life isn't fair, nor was it ever meant to be? Who else but a sibling can teach how to play harder, run faster, and think smarter, and if that doesn't work, how to slow others down?

Siblings teach each other language as well as rules: "The word is not *keputz*," a know-it-all older sister was heard insisting loudly to her younger brother at a fast-food restaurant, "it's kep-shit!" And she dumped some on his French fries.

Busy parents are urged to be impartial, to give one-on-one attention to each child, to encourage the younger one without holding back the older ones, to arbitrate the fights and teach civil rights as well as table manners –

all of these, even while the parents are still struggling with their own private demons of jealousy, impossible impositions, and stifling roles thrust upon them by their siblings.

Sometimes, as in my children's family, there is a special case. I have already said that my youngest son is brain-damaged. (I told his story in *The Book of Matthew*.) I remember when I came home from a grueling diagnostic test Matt had undergone (and failed) being greeted by his sister Liz with the news that she had won a city art contest. It was good news but fraught with danger – for me. Half the trick for a parent is not to lean too hard on other children's successes as compensation so that the children feel they have to perform and produce to make up for the damaged one's shortcomings. And half the trick is not to *downplay* their success, thinking to avoid hurting the feelings of the one who can never hope to live up to such high standards, and so deny the achievers their due share of praise.

What I learned was not to be a comparison shopper, to accept each child's achievements for what they were and to expect the best that each child was capable of. What Matt's siblings had to learn was compassion, patience and tolerance. And forgiveness. Siblings learn the meaning of unconditional acceptance for the sole fact that they are family.

Siblings can also learn charm and humor in their family and help each other develop these qualities. It has been noted that families often have the same group sense of humor. As long as it's not at the expense of one particular member all the time, it can be fascinating and fun.

I was only five years old when my father's father died, but I sat at his dinner table most of my formative years. He was a demanding host: he wanted to be entertained at table. Everyone in his family (my father and my aunts and uncles) learned at an early age to tell a good story with a good punch line. Those who weren't telling it were rooting for it, with encouragement and laughter. That same style carried over into family gatherings long after my grandfather was gone. I sometimes wonder if one of the subliminal reasons I married my husband was that my grandfather would have enjoyed him. Bill was a good dinner partner. Laughter is good relish for any meal whether it's company or family.

Other group lessons that siblings teach include dancing and ball throwing and even (sometimes!) arithmetic, with built-in teachers on hand. They develop their own kind of shorthand with each other. I've known siblings with secret codes, passwords and elaborate plans to defeat the enemy (usually the enemy is US). I've seen siblings in a family, including mine, band together in times of adversity and rally round the parent (me) with a fortitude and wisdom it would be impossible to buy. Human siblings are almost like the Midwych cuckoos in John Wyndham's novel of the same name, so uncanny are they in their organic communication and self-protection. As a team, Liz and her sister Kate can still beat anyone at Charades because they know what the other one is thinking almost before the thought has formed. But they are also disparate. We all are and if we learn it first in families, we'll be stronger for it.

"Make her stop teasing me!" is still a cry from younger siblings everywhere, as they learn devious ways of getting the better of the bigger, smarter one. There may be internal squabbles and resentment, but usually the family is united against the outside world. In a nurturing family they learn to be themselves, but they also learn the satisfaction of being loyal to and responsible for others, and of being trusted to carry out those responsibilities. They learn self-esteem not only from their parents' expectations and praise but also from their siblings' appreciation of them – if they're lucky, and if they give it back. In short, they learn solidarity. One for all and all for one. Brotherhood.

Much as I hate the sexist language of the term, it is an example of an idea that may fade from use along with sisterhood, blood brother, sisters under the skin, fraternity – all because the reality it is based on no longer exists: an abundance of siblings. Maybe nepotism will die! At any rate, it's possible that family connections and loyalties will lose their strength if there are fewer people to whom one owes that kind of devotion. The blood that used to be thicker than water will run thinner and thinner from generation to generation, if, in fact, it regenerates at all.

To sum it up: the family is the crucible where siblings learn their first lessons about the unfairness of life, the value of an ally, the skills of negotiation, and the importance of loyalty. What will happen when these lessons are no longer learned because there's only one child? Where does the child learn how to fight and make up, to share, to survive, to love, and to be responsible for others if there are no others? Maybe life is easier if no favorites are around to be played, but is it real?

In China, it is reported, the only (male) child in each family, because of the one-child-to-a-family government ruling, is growing up spoiled and catered to beyond what is good for his character. With only one child there is no necessity to share. These Little Emperors are now being sent to summer camps where they can experience some of the competition and give-and-take of group living. They may in time change the entire nation's attitude to communism. They have certainly skewed marriage patterns. Eligible young men now outnumber marriageable women by a million. It hasn't strengthened the position of females in the country; they just get a higher bride price for their families as they are sold to the highest bidders, usually older men who can afford to pay more.

There are some aspects of family behavior that may become obsolete without living examples to teach it. What happens to all those metaphors – brotherliness, sisterliness, he/she has been like a brother/sister to me? What happens to fraternal societies and orders upon which many unions are based, or to family companies (Jones & Sons; Smith & Daughter)? What happens to the whole idea of brother/sisterhood when every family has, at most, one lonely, only child? We don't have the answers yet, because the returns aren't in.

Poor lonely, only child, though – or so the myth goes – with no one to play with, pampered and indulged, even spoiled to unrealistic expectations, though neglected by the adults who are too intent on their own lives to pay attention to the child.

Not so, say only children; it's not like that at all. For one thing, I was told, they don't get spoiled, or at least, not indulged. Since an only child is the only one to do the family proud, expectations of performance are higher than normal. In the event of failure, blame is focused rather harshly, and there is no one to share that searing limelight. This has an effect. Certainly the incidence of achievers among only (or eldest) children is very high.

An only child told me she was never neglected or ignored by her parents. Far from it. They included her in their activities from an early age. I see this now among the young families I know. Only children get taken everywhere because it's cheaper than leaving them home with a sitter. Such children quickly learn to behave well and develop a poise far beyond their years. As Benjamin Spock, the guru of my time, said, "Perhaps a child who is fussed over gets a feeling of destiny, he thinks he is in the world for something important and it gives him drive and confidence." That's not to say it's impossible to impart this confidence to younger children.

As for the give-and-take of sibling rivalry, I am told that the only child gets that in day care now. Surveys indicate that day-care children demonstrate a far greater degree of sociability and cooperation (also aggressiveness) at an earlier age than stay-at-home children. It doesn't matter whether they are only children or have siblings, they develop group responses when exposed to the give-and-take of day care. Nor is day care the only group activity that provides the single child with the experience of getting along with other children. As they get older they can join organized sports and other activities, all

involving group cooperation, as well as summer camps, both boarding and day. In fact, these days, very few young people are alone for
long at whatever age. They seem to be processed in herds and to
move in packs and to find their stability and self-image among their
peers – great crowds of them.

Canadian families are having one, at most two, children, and some of
them worry that they are depriving their children of the camaraderie of
their own families. We have reached the point where most children today
have more parents and grandparents than they do siblings, especially if
there is a divorce (or two) in the family. Canada's birthrate has fallen to
the point where we are no longer producing enough children to replace
ourselves. New citizens are going to have to come from elsewhere,
through immigration.

Lonely or only, children will find companions. Nature abhors a vacuum.
When all my children's grandparents but one died, my husband's maiden
aunt married at the age of 65 thus bringing two surrogate grandparents into
our lives: doting, fussy, kind people who attended the children's Christmas
concerts and music recitals, took them to movies and fed them too much
candy and admired everything they did. As the saying goes, when a door
closes, a window opens.

I see today's young parents sharing child care, excursions and special
events with their own siblings and their children. In other words, cousins
enjoy a larger family life. The advantage to this is that cousins can be the
same age and same sex, something that is possible within a nuclear family
only in the case of twins. The other advantage is that cousins go away, back
to their own homes, so that little girls don't have to put up with whiny little
boys or bullying big ones, and little boys don't have to be nice all the time
to nagging little girls or stop tattling on know-it-all big ones. It's easier to
ignore a cousin, so they get the pleasure of being almost like siblings without the infighting.

If there aren't any cousins to bring together, young families can import a playmate for an only child to take along to the zoo or a picnic or a fair so there is a companion to share the festivities; a young guest can be invited for a week at a cottage with the family, or on a special excursion for a long weekend. Often such a favor is returned, so that the parents get a weekend off. Lots of combinations are possible and are practiced.

Lonely only children aren't the only ones who don't have built-in companions. There are other kinds of "only" children. They used to be known as afterthoughts: surprise babies born late in the life of mature parents who thought they were past that sort of thing. These occur now more frequently not by accident but by design when a divorced older man has married a younger woman who wants a child of her own. There is also the "only" child born to remarried parents who each has a child/children from a former marriage but who want a child of their new union. In these cases, isolation by age may make the child seem only, though he or she may have half-brothers or -sisters, or steps-. The combinations these days are mind boggling without even mentioning the only children of same-sex marriages, who may or may not be the biological offspring of one of the parents.

I talked to a number of parents of the "only" child in a blended family. Many of them have confessed to me what seemed to them an insurmountable problem they couldn't correct. They loved their own child, the fruit of the new union, more than they cared for the others, particularly the others from the spouse's previous marriage. It's understandable, blood and genes being what they are.

But here is a new danger, a new source of rivalry and jealousy for the new generation. Whom does mother love best now? The circumstances may be different, but the emotion is the same. How are families dealing with it?

As one mother put it, "I may feel like hitting the others, but I clout my own."

That's favoritism?

THE SANDWICH GENERATION

They launch, and they come home again.
– Rachel Schlesinger

The human young are unique in the animal world for the length of time they require to mature and function independently of their parents. These days it takes longer because even when the parents think they're out of the nest for good and all, they're not. They come home again.

Know-it-all sociologists talk about the Empty Nest Syndrome and how hard it is on parents, especially mothers who are supposed to consider themselves out of a job. Much they know. Most women who reach this stage are delighted to get the kids off their hands. I have to qualify that: that is, if they are still married and facing the sunset years with a life companion. After losing my husband, I must admit to feeling a further loss of identity to have my children peel away, the last two in the same year. I needn't have worried. I hadn't seen the last of them, and I am not unique in my experience. According to the 1994 Canada census, over a million children over the age of 18 were living at home with their families of origin. The Old Folks are definitely not alone.

Dr. Robert Glossop of the VIF has listed the most significant reasons for this continuing social phenomenon (with my comments and elaboration).

➤ Education. It takes longer and costs more to get one these days, but without it there's small hope of being financially independent. In the meantime, free (?) room and board at home is very handy.

➤ The economy. The kid might have a job, but not usually a high-paying, top-executive slot. In fact, the remuneration is quite modest, not to say meager, and food and rent cost more than expected. I've seen kids, including my own, come home for a while until they get a stake.

➤ Unemployment. Just because they have a job doesn't mean they'll keep it. We all know about the unemployment rate these days. McJobs are not the answer either. I've seen young men busy with résumés and interviews waiting in a safe, cheap refuge – their parent's home – until the right job came along.

➤ Marriage postponement. People are delaying marriage a little longer; while they wait, they tarry a little longer at home. Statistics indicate that 14 percent of women and 17 percent of men will never marry, figures that are up by six or seven percentage points since the 1970s. Where are they living?

➤ Births to unwed mothers. One survey concluded that about half of all unwed mothers take their babies home for at least the first two years. I knew the parents of a young unmarried woman who brought her baby home for her mother to care for while she continued her education. The girl's parents were just on the point of retiring, looking forward to freedom and travel, and then they were stuck with another child – not that they didn't love her. It's still happening in different contexts. Most recently I met a woman who cared for twin toddlers while her son and daughter-in-law were breaking up. The sad ending is that when the split was final, the mother got custody and the paternal grandmother no longer sees her darling grandchildren.

➤ The high divorce rate. In my day, "going home to mother" used to be a joke. Now it's no joke. Between marriages, home is a nice place to go, especially if there are children and free baby-sitting is thrown in (see above). That's what grandparents are for, right?

As a matter of fact, most grandparents are finding it necessary to set a time limit on the return to the nest. As one grandmother put it, referring to the night crying of her grandchild, "I can't take any more. I no longer have the patience." Sometimes once was enough. Visits are one thing. Wholesale invasion is quite another. Most children, once they leave their family of origin, become alien.

On the other hand, what about the poor, out-of-luck, stranded, abandoned adult child? Being a Grey Eminence with a checkered past, I have the dubious distinction of having seen both sides.

We did it to my parents. We had two very young children and were ready to move into a house when our mortgage arrangements fell through and we had to build a house, which wouldn't be ready for six months. We had already given notice on the duplex we were living in and we had no place to go. We moved in with my family of origin.

Suddenly I was the child again, dependent once more on my parents. Though I had been married and running my own household for six years, I stopped thinking. I couldn't plan meals, I didn't seem to be able to function. Sex, need I say, was difficult; I felt virginal, guilty, and afraid to make any noise. (Nevertheless, I managed to get pregnant again.)

Manitoba's liquor laws had just changed, and Winnipeg was opening its first licensed bars that summer. My husband and I tried them all, one by one as they opened, taking advantage of free baby sitters. We celebrated the framing in, the wiring, the plastering, every stage of our house as it became ready to receive us. It was a chance to get out of my parental house and talk.

Years later, I was in an apartment when it happened to me as a parent and, though it was only for a brief time, it felt like slum living while we went through it. My youngest was still at home, taking longer to leave; my next youngest lived at home while working at his summer jobs between university years – so that was only four or five months – but there was an overlap because my next up returned broke from Europe and I gave her room and board until she found a job. Suddenly I was planning meals again, juggling schedules other than my own, handling more laundry and finding the voice I thought I had forgotten how to raise. I had one advantage, if it can be called that: I was widowed, and I really enjoyed my children's company.

There's another aspect to this extended family trend, and that is the increasing dependency of the senior generation. More and more frequently now, as more people are living longer, aging parents are outliving if not their money, at least their strength, and cannot cope by themselves. Married people seem to manage longer, but even so, one hears of couples so old and frail they can't help each other and must be separated in long-term care or nursing homes. More common, however, is an aging, widowed mother who needs a safe place to live or at least people to help her stay in her own home. More often than not, the caregiver is a woman, whether daughter or daughter-in-law.

The people caught in the middle, squeezed between still-dependent young adults and failing seniors, have become known as The Sandwich Generation. It's an aspect of family life that never existed before. We talk of the past with misty-eyed, uninformed nostalgia for the times when three generations lived happily under one roof. It didn't happen; young people of an earlier generation married younger, left, and stayed married. As for the old folks, they didn't used to live that long. Men as well as women are living longer these days.

One futurist suggested that the way to get around the imbalance of male-female population in the upper age range would be to institute polygamy, that is, for one man to have two or more wives. Quite apart from any moral objections current in our society, which allows only serial wives, not concurrent ones, it wouldn't work. Women share kitchens even less well than they share men. Bathrooms are even more sacrosanct.

But what do we do? Once we women reach a certain age, nothing seems to stop us except rot. A woman who is 65 today can expect to live at least another 19 years and a man almost 15, if he eats his vegetables; if a woman is 86 today she has a 50–50 chance of living another six and a half years.

Gloria Steinem and I intend to live until we're 97, but we may change our minds. Some younger women are trying to reduce their odds by smoking, thereby increasing their chance of lung cancer over that of men.

By the time women reach their 60s, three-quarters of them are single, for whatever reason, but they don't want to live with their children if they can help it. The feeling is mutual. Still, one bows eventually to the inevitable as husbands and strength and marbles leave. Older men, the ones who have survived, are more usually living with their wives, but sooner or later, they too face solitude, though of course in lesser numbers. However, we are not yet a nation of institutions. Family remains important.

A low percentage, under 10 percent, of seniors under 85 are living in institutions (nursing homes, long-term care hospitals, etc.); over 85 the picture changes. From 25 percent (men) to 30 percent (women) of these senior seniors live in institutions. The majority of older single people live with one or more relatives, either blood- or marriage-related – in other words: family.

This is now. This is not forever. Forever is up there in the 21st century; by the year 2030 the number of people over 65 will comprise almost 25 percent of the population. All it takes is time.

This scenario frightens the Boomers, the oldest of whom will be reaching retirement age in 15 years, or sooner as enforced early retirement becomes more common. Having been the squeezed filling, they're fearful of what will happen when they become the outside crust on that squeezed sandwich. They're declaring emphatically that their kids aren't going to have to look after them, that they're going to stay independent in their old age. It's a good thing they feel that way, because they don't have enough kids to fall back on, anyway. They're making lots of financial plans for their twilight years, although they haven't given much thought to their emotional future, the human side of the grim statistics that financial planners keep hurling at them. Family keeps on being important, whether they're live-in, live-out, close neighbors or arm's length.

The most pressing current problem is what is happening to grandparents when there is a divorce in the family. Just because a mate has been exed doesn't mean the grandparents have to disappear, but that is often what happens. When it comes to divorce, people take very short views; they think they're dealing with only two generations. They're not. When one or the other side of the family sinks into oblivion, that's not only unfair to the children, it's heartbreaking to the grandparents (see custody, p. 188).

Everyone needs nurturing, especially children and especially children from split families, but grandparents suffer too. In the case of sole custody, the parents of the barred parent often get completely shortchanged and never see the children from one year to the next. It's not only the grandparents who are troubled. With the personnel changing in children's lives, it would be nice if they could count on a few old, loving faces and a place that is familiar to them. Children can be very comforted by an elder whose love and domicile hasn't changed. One little boy summed up his domestic arrangements to his grandmother after his parents split: "I have three beds now," he said to his grandmother. "I have a bed at my mom's and a bed at my dad's and my bed here with you."

Slightly older children will often keep in touch with their grandparents by themselves. When the world as they knew it has come crashing down around their Walkmans, teenagers especially may find a grandparent a real source of comfort and understanding. Younger children may have to be helped to keep in touch, no matter whose parents the grand ones are, and no matter who has access. The world keeps changing, and we with it.

I read of a man who received an emergency phone call from a teenager and rushed to help. The boy was the son of the man's first wife's husband – no blood relation at all, but kin all the same. The case for grandparents is stronger than that. They are, after all, related by blood.

In any case, grandparents should continue to be included in family gatherings and be apprised of family news and events. The adult children are not without their own pain and the senior parents can sometimes help, if given a chance. We need all the nurturers we can get.

In the case of geographic absence, a different effort has to be made to achieve some kind of closeness of the heart. The long distance phone commercials at Christmas always put a lump in my throat because they're so true. There's also a little thing called a tape recorder. I know grandparents who tell or read stories to their grandchildren on tape and mail the cassettes. These days even greater electronic wonders are at our frail fingertips: faxes and e-mail. I have received faxed stories and drawings from my grandchildren and I'm getting around to an e-mail address, not as cosy as a fireplace to curl up by to tell stories, but the next best thing to being there.

Speaking of stories, that's one of the things grandparents are supposed to be for. Even ones who are not gifted at storytelling can enthrall a young child and interest a curious older one with stories of the "olden days." Some high schools assign the gathering of such stories before they disappear with the old-timers (or with Alzheimers?).

I have been collecting women's diaries for several years, fascinated by the different uses people have for them, including archival. I met one grandmother, not a writer, who is making it the last work of her life to describe one day in her life. This is not as simple as it sounds. She had been working on it for about three years when I met her, and she was only up to midmorning. She is describing and explaining everything: décor, texture, assumptions, habits, sources and so on. It took her pages, she said, to describe the bed and its fittings: sheets, pillows, electric blanket, mattress, box spring, and so on. That is a very detailed kind of storying.

That woman's "day" should be a useful social document, not only for her grandchildren but for historians in the future.

After I met that woman, I came across another diarist who was also addressing her grandchildren – one, actually – her as-yet unborn granddaughter. (She was certain the child, not even conceived when she began writing, was going to be a girl, and it was.) Ethel Robertson Whiting's intention, as she begins her diary on March 11, 1924, at the age of 42, is to leave a written record for her as yet unborn granddaughter, and she warns her: "You won't want me for an ancestor," but proceeds to disprove it with her charm and candor even though she is only a wife and mother.

> *Cooking, walking the floor with sleepless babies, nursing sick children, is not sensational work. It can be done by tender, loving, capable – But alas! tiresome women.*
>
> *Whereas it is beyond imagination that a tiresome person could be Secretary to the Caliph of Bagdad.*
>
> *What we need is a publicity agent to dramatize our activities.**

Elise Boulding is a sociologist much quoted by the VIF. She coined the term *nurturance* to make a noun of the kind of care that families give one another, too often left to the women to perform. We all need nurturing, male and female, and we all have to supply it to each other. The more practice we have, the better we get at it – spreading the sandwich bread with love.

Society as a whole has always tended to move back and forth between close, tight, protective support of the family unit and the looser, wide-ranging network of the community, often balancing one against

---

* quoted from the diary of Ethel Robertson Whiting, in *Private Pages: Diaries of American Women, 1830s–1970s*, ed. Penelope Franklin. Ballantine Books, New York, 1986.

the other. One of the most difficult aspects of the nuclear family has been its singularity, the expectation that it would achieve for its members what larger kin groups and communities have done in the past. Now, as the family gets smaller and smaller, it must acknowledge the value of the elders within its midst.

It may also have to turn back to the community. Can the community at large take the responsibility? Can it stand the strain? Will society provide the necessary support? Without kin, we're all going to have to learn how to be kind.

As American feminist writer Letty Cottin Pogrebin puts it, "All we have are love and time."

And as the poet W.H. Auden put it, "We must love one another or die."

5

What's the Magic Word?

The great secret of morals is love.
– Percy Bysshe Shelley

MANNERS AND MORALS

It is not by accident that I lump manners and morals together. They both begin on a very simple level, based on the Golden Rule, which itself translates almost word for word into the creeds of the major world religions. Manners teach a sensitivity for others' feelings and suggest some guidelines for protecting them. Morals take over from manners for the big stuff, but they boil down (up) to the same thing: being responsible for and caring about other people's well-being, that is, loving your neighbor as yourself.

Most people learn their manners, or lack of them, in their family of origin. We all know that, like it or not, our children's behavior reflects on their parents – especially Mom. Fathers usually take responsibility for more "important" behavior, such as physical prowess or courage and good grades, which reminds me of a nice line of Robert Frost:

> *You don't have to deserve your mother's love.*
> *You have to deserve your father's.*
> *He's more particular.*

Although I'm not sure it's true. Children, if they're lucky, are taught their manners at an early age. What, exactly, have they learned? The question is, have their parents been courteous to them?

Another word for manners is etiquette, which people tend to shy away from, thinking it's for sissies and snobs with all its la-de-da rules about when and how to curtsy and which fork to use first at a formal dinner and what to call the Queen if ever they should meet. All etiquette – or courtesy, or manners – really is, is consideration. Consideration simply means that one doesn't eat with one's hands or pick one's nose in public for fear of offending someone else. Somewhere along the way some of the rules got a little refined; not eating with one's hands is one thing, the correct choice of a plethora of forks is carrying it further than most people ever need to, if only because they don't own that many. It helps children as they grow older if they have learned the basic rules, and gives them that magic thing called poise. That's another function that families perform: they teach their members how to behave in public.

Erving Goffman called it "the presentation of self" in a book that calls into question what exactly we are presenting. Families govern one's public presentation in many ways that we are not even fully conscious of. We should learn to distinguish the ways and to lay blame or praise where it is due without falling into yet another swamp of stereotypes. Whose fault is it if the clothes fade because of the soap guess-who is using? Although the television commercials sometimes bring the man into play – scrubbing the bathtub in order to get a little R&R in same with the wife he has helped – we all still somehow know whose fault it is if the kids or house are dirty.

And if the children don't behave well, who agonizes more? Who remembers the dates of the birthdays, anniversaries and milestones, not only of the children but of the grandparents – on both sides of the family? Who wraps the presents? Who bakes (or buys) the brownies for the school meeting? Who knows the family's allergies – including either spouse's siblings and someone's maiden aunt – and plans around them at family feasts? Who keeps track of the doctors' and other appointments? Who doesn't like Brussels sprouts, and who remembers who doesn't? Who darns the socks? (Nobody!) Who knows where the prescriptions are filed, including for glasses as well as those allergies?

I will not pause for the answers but go on to some one-sided dialogue in case any of it sounds familiar.

➤ You are not leaving this house looking like that!

➤ Always wear clean underwear in case you have an accident and have to go to the hospital.

➤ What's Melanie's mother going to think if she sees you wearing that ratty old sweater?

➤ You're not going anywhere until you clean up.

➤ I'm not going to be seen with you until you get a haircut.

➤ No one comes to the table in my house without a shirt on.

➤ The least you could do is shave when we have company coming.

➤ The guest towels are for the guests.

➤ Please don't eat the daisies.

There is no prize for the correct answer. No one wins. No matter whose responsibility it ultimately is, our families teach us what appearances to foster, what behavior to endorse. Unspoken rules in every family somehow, without ever being spelled out, tell us what is and isn't acceptable behavior (particularly in the areas of sexual activity and incest, the most common taboos).

Apart from the general rules, most of us, as I have already mentioned, have been given a role to play within the family, not always realistic or consistent with the truth as we see it. Sometimes, but not always, the role our family gives us is the first role we play in public, although it may not be the last one. Thus a bright girl may be required to hide her intelligence to appear less capable than she really is. A gentle boy may be forced to put on a macho exterior to protect himself from ridicule. Fathers who know best have been allowed to think so by deceptive wives who make all the decisions and do all the work behind the scenes, giving their husbands nothing to do but grant smiling approval. And klutzy women are revered and honored because they're so kind and bumbling and never critical. Present-day ideals of partnership require other performances, perhaps not yet perfected by either party: Good Ol' Dad, Super Mom, Sensitive Man, Ms. Efficiency, Macho Stud.

"All the world's a stage," said Shakespeare, but we're not all players, not all the time; I hope not all the time. The family teaches us our first lines, that is, our manners, the learned techniques by which we get along with others. What we do with them after that depends on a number of things: nerve, confidence, self-discipline, character and luck. The luck comes first, if we had parents who tried to teach us something worthwhile. We see in nightly headlines the catastrophic, often fatal results of undisciplined behavior in untaught, amoral children.

Before we blame families for this, we must ask: is it entirely their fault? Surely the community must take some responsibility for the factors that contribute to someone's losing the way? These days we can hardly begin to discuss family without broadening the focus to politics. R. D. Laing titled one of his books *The Politics of the Family* and meant the interaction of its members, but it could well be another discussion entirely and deal with income, housing, education, opportunity, Medicare, welfare, protection, security, on and on, because the priorities of the community affect the functioning of the family. Choices are hierarchical and have a trickle-down effect.

Situational ethics is the name given to a subject that has actually been finding its way into school curricula. Hypothetical situations are presented to students, who must then decide on an appropriate response. Example: a group of tourists are trapped in a cave with an escape hatch through a crawl space large enough to admit one person at a time. There is enough air to last about two hours and the chance that a further rock slide will seal in the occupants forever. The class has to decide who goes first, and the subsequent order of escape. Titanic, anyone?

Other similar no-win situations are offered and demand discussion about ethical behavior, not to mention negotiation and manipulation. There are no prizes but a revelation about what is prized. Who goes first: The children, a.k.a. the future? Mothers and teachers, who safeguard that future? The tycoons who contribute jobs to the community? The caregivers (i.e. social workers, doctors, ministers) who take care of the community?

What else is family but a continuing series of ethical, not to say political, situations? What better place, then, to learn how to deal with situational society and to make mistakes that are not, at first, irrevocable? A family situation is usually, supposedly, a forgiving one, if only because the members have to go on living with each other. Sometimes things happen when they can't; sometimes things happen that everyone must ignore and keep secret. Playwrights find half their plots and all their characters in families.

Situational society is less forgiving. It offers very few exits or compromises. Ideally, the family allows its members, while learning about life, to try many doors. Ideally also, the family teaches its members basic morality, although some families have a little trouble these days distinguishing between being "nice" and being good.

Many people think sin is just an acronym for their social insurance number. The still, small voice of conscience that was supposed to prevent people from doing wrong is stiller and smaller than it ever was, if it even exists, and it is drowned out by all sorts of rationalization and justification.

➤ Everybody does it.

➤ They had it coming to them.

➤ If I don't do it, someone else will.

➤ I've had a hard life, I deserve a break.

➤ I've been good for a long time, I need a holiday.

➤ No one will notice.

➤ I'll make up for it.

And here's an increasingly frequent one.

➤ I saw it in a movie.

As major deterrents to immoral, antisocial behavior, church and school have fallen away. Canada is not considered to be a Christian country any more and other religions have not replaced the Judeo-Christian ethic. More and more schools are producing their pageants at festival times of the year based on the winter solstice or spring rites or on lay celebrations like Halloween or Valentine's Day, once religious in their own right but subsumed by Hallmark. This, of course, is so as not to offend the ethnic mix in the schools now, and not all bad, of course. The world is smaller but holds many rooms.

According to moral tales of earlier decades – one thinks of Victorian samplers and uplifting children's stories – it was the memory of Mother's voice or the thought of Father's disappointment that kept people on the straight and narrow, just as in earlier centuries it was the threat of fire and brimstone that (sometimes) stopped an evil deed. Now with the fears of a literal hell long allayed, and the sound of Mother's voice and Father's pronouncements as still as the small one within, what's to stop people from doing wrong, from harming society?

Right-wing conservatives are calling for stricter rules and harsher punishments and seem unable to see a relationship between the number of Food Banks in the country, and the million or so children who use them, and the future of the family.

Right – the family. The family is still almost the only consistent, built-in source of moral education. It continues to instill some system of checks and balances in its members before they run rampant in society. The system of inculcation may begin with ritual and manners, but it culminates in morality.

As Robert Glossop has said, "We are beginning to remember that family is a stronger agent in the educational process than the schools, a stronger teacher of values than the church, and a stronger influence on the socialization process of children than the media." I do hope the latter is true. V-chips are not the answer.

It therefore behooves parents to realize what their own values are and to figure out how to communicate them to their children, and then, how to help their children internalize them. It seems to me that sometimes parents are more worried about their children swallowing their vitamin pills than their morals. Perhaps it was easier when the church was there to help, but the patriarchal system hasn't done anyone much good, especially mothers. So where does that leave us? What are the intrinsic and moral values we want to pass along to our children?

These are not a matter of personal preference, and they are not open to negotiation. There really is a world- and time- honored standard, certain basic, self-evident truths about human rights and dignity and freedom. There are also time-tested personal standards of behavior that children might as well learn, things like honesty and truthfulness (not the same thing), self-control, fidelity and loyalty (also not the same thing), a sense of justice and a sense of fair play. It really can be condensed into what Shelley and Auden, as well as other geniuses like Christ and Mohammed, have said: love.

I don't really think much of St. Paul's male chauvinist attitudes but what he had to say about love is still valid:

> *Love is patient and kind; it is not jealous, or conceited, or proud; love is not ill-mannered, or selfish, or irritable; love does not keep a record of wrongs; love is not happy with evil, but is happy with the truth. Love never gives up; and its faith, hope and patience never fail... these three remain: faith, hope, and love, and the greatest of these is love.*
>
> – 1 Corinthians 13:4–13

No one ever said it was easy.

6

Nice Girls/Boys Don't

When all is said and done, discretion is what counts.
– Alice Leone Moats,
from *No Nice Girl Swears*
(a book of etiquette published in 1933)

WHO'S WATCHING?

In the last chapter, I came perilously close to touching on this one, when I wondered where the still small voice comes from that controls behavior. Then I was considering the source of teaching, or its lack, and of morality in general. But what about actual behavior? Apart from wondering where a standard of values or morals comes from and how it is instilled, I also wonder how it translates into action. This is hands-on situational ethics now – individual responses to specific situations.

There are enough broad similarities in a family's problems that I can describe a general approach to them rather than try to deal with one or two anecdotes. The teenager with a good-paying part-time job who is feeling very independent and wonders why he still has to obey the rules has more in common than would seem to be the case with his little sister, who is bargaining for free-range rights on her bicycle; with his father, whose pressures at work make him feel he's justified for sloughing off some of his family duties; and with his mother who threatens to go on strike because, while also carrying an outside job, she feels like the drudge who has to do everything at home.

People want to know what to tell their children about sex, why they can't watch certain TV programs or movies, how to handle allowances, why grandparents can't understand how little time they have to visit, where they can save money in a dwindling economy (theirs), and who's listening, anyway? The problems are myriad and specific, but the approach to most of them can be generalized and spelled out. What is really helpful is some preventive care – like preventive housekeeping where the problem/clutter/dirt is stopped before it has a chance to settle.

The key to solving most of these problems is respect. Here, from the *Gage Canadian Dictionary* are the definitions of respect as they concern us, along with the sample sentences to illustrate nuances:

(noun)

1. *honor; esteem:* Children should show respect for those who are older and wiser.

2. *consideration; regard:* Show respect for other people's property.

(verb)

1. *feel or show honor or esteem for:* We respect an honest person.

2. *show consideration for:* Respect the ideas and feelings of others.

3. *relate to; refer to; be connected with.*

(syn.)

Respect, regard = consideration, felt or shown, for someone or something of recognized worth or value.

Respect emphasizes recognizing or judging the worth or value of someone or something and paying the consideration or honor due: A soldier may feel respect for an officer he dislikes.

Regard emphasizes seeing that a person or thing is entitled to consideration, appreciation, or admiration, and usually suggests a kindly, friendly, or sympathetic feeling: A person who reads another's mail has no regard for other people's privacy.

I couldn't have chosen the examples better if I'd written them myself! Isn't it amazing what one can learn from dictionaries?

I have a single friend whose teenage son had a part-time job. One day he announced to her that he was going to skip school the next day and go cruising with his friends. At least he told her. One of the sad advantages of being a single parent is that her children talk to her more and she listens more. My friend said she didn't approve of skipping school, on principle. Her son said he'd been very good, needed a break, and besides, she'd let him skip school for a swimming meet out of town, why couldn't he skip again for R&R?

My friend looked up at her son, who towered over her, and wondered what to say.

"Look," she said, "I can't hit you, because you're bigger than I am."

"You never did," said her son.

"I know." She continued, "I can't stop your allowance because you earn your own money. I can't refuse to write you a note to excuse your absence, because you're beyond that sort of thing now. I can't squeal on you because what good will that do, and I hate squealers."

She looked at him. He waited.

"All I can say is, I don't like it. You must honor your commitments. Right now your commitment is to school. I'm just telling you what I think is best. You have to do what you think is best."

There was a brief silence.

"I'll go to school," her son said. That boy's decision, I think, was made years before.

The reason I know that story so well is that I was the single parent and the boy was my son. He still amazes me.

There are lots of times when a family member runs into direct conflict with one's mate, parents, or siblings, when there are two opposing points of view – lucky if there are only two! How do they resolve their differences and still smile at each other over breakfast (*no one* smiles at breakfast!) – or, if not smile, at least not growl? Again, respect.

The problem is more often one of negotiation rather than of communication. If respect for the other's point of view is present, then at least a dialogue can be established. Families have to learn to win some, lose some, to give and take – and to know the difference between giving and taking. Treaties and agreements are as important as briefs and hearings. (Maybe one member of the family will grow up to be a strike negotiator.)

We used to have very loud family discussions, not angry, just loud. I remember one time on vacation when my mother was with us, we were having a family discussion about what to do that day. Everyone had a plan and was trying to convince the others of the wisdom of it. My mother started to cry and left the room saying she couldn't bear to hear us fight. We were all astonished.

"We weren't fighting," I explained. "We were having a discussion." Very healthy.

The strength of open family discussions is the opportunity it provides for total involvement. (See "Holding a Family Council," pp. 228–230.) No one within a family can change without the whole family changing. Often one member's problem will turn out to be caused by several members' behavior patterns. When this is recognized, then all members must agree to modify their behavior if effective change is to take place.

The problem at hand may be something as simple as being late for school, but it is a problem because it involves detentions, delays, and so on. Say Debbie likes to wash her hair every morning but Alex always beats her into the bathroom, so she's late. Negotiations and the posting of a schedule – on the bathroom door instead of the fridge door – may resolve the problem, but both parties have to compromise and change. Perhaps D. will wash her hair every other morning or at night, or get up earlier; maybe A. will get an electric razor and shave in his bedroom; maybe the family will install another bathroom – or move! This is why I didn't want to get into specifics. The solutions can be far-reaching.

Obviously, some negotiations must be limited to the members immediately involved, with perhaps a mediator, if necessary (the other parent, or a counselor). Some testimony is too tender and personal to be heard by all, and too shattering for the party to have it aired. Respect, again, is the key word – respect for another's feelings, for dignity, for privacy. Every individual has a safety zone of privacy. Everyone's space should be respected.

Every family, of course, has its own level of reticence: what they are comfortable dealing with out in the open and what they prefer to keep private or secret. There are always subjects better left untouched, but the choice of these is left to each family's threshold of tolerance. Secrets can be healthy and sometimes delicious, as well as destructive. In his book, *The Presentation of Self in Everyday Life*, Erving Goffman thinks that what he calls "points of reticence" play a strong role in a healthy family:

> *In well-adjusted marriages, we expect that each partner may keep from the other secrets having to do with financial matters, past experiences, current flirtations, indulgences in "bad" or expensive habits, personal aspirations and worries, actions of children, true opinions held about relatives or mutual friends, etc.*

On the other hand, in her book *A Chorus of Stones*, American feminist Susan Griffin equates some family secrets with the causes of war. Of course, there are secrets and secrets. She thinks we all become used to "little lies of being" that cause "subtle changes in posture, or dress or speech, to match an occasion at which convention is required, becoming more manly, more ladylike for a period, until, returning home, we feel more ourselves."

But when damaging secrets require other explanations, they become prisons barring us from the truth. She writes: "The stories we tell ourselves, particularly the silent or barely audible ones, are very powerful. They become invisible enclosures."

That's when they become part of the shadow world on the dark side of family life. It will be necessary to redeem it with light.

7

Families at Work

*A job gives a wife clout. Men respect paid employment
outside the home more than they respect housework.*
– quoted from *American Couples*

DOUBLE-INCOME FAMILIES

From one point of view, the so-called nuclear family – bread-winning father, stay-at-home mother, 1.7 children (down from 2.5) – is almost obsolete. If you take Dick out of the tree, put a hockey stick in Jane's hands,
and remove the apron from Mother's waist, the family may seem unclear,
but it's still nuclear. That is, it is the pattern most North Americans grew
up with: a two-generation household with mother and father and their children living under one roof.

You can say anything with statistics. Sure, a horrifying number of children will live with only one parent for some time before they reach their
majority; by the same token, look at the huge numbers who experience what
we still prefer to call a normal home life. There is no doubt, however, that
home life has changed, mainly because no one's at home – during the day.

This is where the staggering statistic comes from when the number crunchers go to count the two-parent families with a stay-at-home mom – that is, families with a single wage earner. Those families now comprise from 4 to 7 percent of the population, depending on which stats you read and which side of the border you're counting on.

In 1994, 52 percent of all women aged 15 and over had jobs, up from 42 percent in 1976. Younger women, married or not, accounted for 70 percent of the employed work force, while 66 percent of those aged 45–54 were employed. The real difference lies in the numbers with children. Between 1981 and 1994, the employment rate of women with children younger than 16 living at home rose from 50 percent to 63 percent, and even those with very young children are on the increase. By 1994, over half (56 percent) of women working outside the home had children under three, up from 39 percent in 1981. I'll tell you one thing: that's an awful lot of tired mothers!

In a majority of these families, the wife's job is necessary for survival, not merely for material goods or an excuse to get out of the house, although her salary continues the myth that men earn a family wage. (As I write this, women's best wage for a full-time job is about 70 percent of a man's. Part-time workers still receive only about 60-63 percent of a man's pay, and 63 percent of part-time workers are women.)

I can't help but notice that a family's needs now are more expensive and varied than they used to be. Bottom line for a lot of people in North America is higher than it was, requiring more material goods, sophisticated food and a greater variety of recreation than earlier generations enjoyed. The good life today is neither simple nor cheap. Reformers who predicted a life of productive leisure for the worker once the 40- (or 35-) hour week was established didn't realize how expensive that leisure time was going to be.

Initially, several centuries ago, the family was a productive unit, meeting its own needs – not just food and supplies, but also clothes, maintenance, implements, and most of the services it required. When the Industrial Revolution moved production out of the home and fields and into offices and factories, the family became more and more a consuming unit, using the products and services supplied by others outside the home. In this change, women especially were deprived of many traditional roles: not merely those of brewer, baker, educator of children and servants, but also manufacturer of clothes, plus healer, caregiver, midwife (a specialty taken over by certain women in the community), and layer-out of the dead. What a woman became by Victorian times was (already noted) the Angel of the House – *Mother*.

Also Consumer. Someone had to buy and use all those things that were being produced for families. Personal consumption became a way of life; it was time-consuming, hard work, and very good for the economy. In an essay on the family in *A History of Private Life: Riddles of Identity in Modern Times*, Elaine Taylor May reports:

> *The amount spent nationally for personal consumption nearly tripled between 1908 and 1929, with the most striking increase for clothes, personal care, furniture, appliances, cars, and recreation – primarily activities and goods associated with private life. Mass consumption offered the promise – or the illusion – that the good life was within everyone's reach.*

And, in fact, it was. As production and wages went up the blue-collar worker entered the middle class and started accumulating things, spending money on leisure activities, even taking vacations.

After World War II the drive for accumulation reached frenzied proportions; not only were Mixmasters and fridges available again, they came in assorted colors. Women who may have worked outside the home to help the war effort were told to go home and let the returning men have their jobs back. The 1940s and 1950s, when all those babies started being born, saw a return to Victorian ideals, a postwar dream which frayed as the sharp edge of economic reality began to saw away at it. It was no longer possible to keep that bubble afloat without two incomes; the so-called breadwinner's alone was not enough.

North Americans have become consumers and hedonists, all wanting to live the good life, unwilling to put off any present or instant gratification for future satisfaction or security. The good life costs: gourmet cooking with trendy foods, wine with dinner every night – not only for special, rare occasions – Sunday brunch, spectator sports, theater performances, concerts, jogging, snow and water sports and travel, all captured in photographs or in moving, talking pictures, with the appropriate clothes and equipment for all these activities. Expensive.

So Mother went out to work, but not only for the goodies. If all the women working outside the home quit tomorrow, the number of families living below the Low Income Cut-Off (this is what Statistics Canada euphemistically calls the poverty line) would double. So what happened to the great leisurely weekend? Truth is, the double-income family is so busy earning the money for it that it doesn't have time to enjoy it. I'm talking about families with children. Each day starts early, finding clean clothes for everyone, packing lunches, driving little ones to day care, preparing for work. At the other end, it's pick-up time, a few wash loads, something for dinner (and if someone forgot to thaw something, it's fast-food: take-out or microwave), dishes, bath time, story, TV or homework (for adults as well as children), early exhaustion. Weekends are for errands, groceries, renovations, chauffeuring to hockey, swimming, ballet, baton practice. Have I mentioned TV? Yes. Videos? Nintendo? A boon or a bane.

The wife and mother who works outside the home works an estimated 60-70 hour week. She has actually cut her former housework time by about 10-15 hours a week, but she's working double time now. The husband whose wife goes to work, while he *participates* in family chores, increases his share of the actual housework an average of four hours a week, a little better than the nine extra minutes a day of ten years ago. Working wives and mothers enjoy fewer leisure hours than anyone (another survey), including their husbands. A kind of madness has everyone on a treadmill; it's called overwork and yet most of these busy women do not suffer burn out. They're just tired, that's all. There aren't enough hours in the day. Something has to give. And a lot does.

Like the cleaning, bed-making, mending, a lot of the cooking, social life and volunteer work, story time. The children sometimes get shortchanged. "If only," wailed one mother, "I could send the children out with the shirts."

Before anyone gets too dismayed, we should remember that people used to do just that – send the kids out. Babies were sent out to wet nurses (and most of them died); boys were sent out to castles, or smithies, or boarding schools. No one expected one woman to bring up children all by herself and no woman did. Never in history have parents and children been so close, even with all this busy-ness. Quantity time there isn't; quality time is maybe not quite as qualitative as it used to be but was it ever?

Men, of course, have their own balancing act to tend to. They also experience this home/work juggling routine, though not to the same extent that women do. I have interviewed couples who spell each other off. The men work night or flexible shifts and then go home and take over when the women start their day, ships passing each other in the night, with scarcely a minute to pass on essential information, let alone spend meaningful time together, or sleep.

As a writer, I have known a number of men who are artists (writers, composers, painters) and who work at home, or at least outside regular offices and hours. A composer I worked with on a project was an effective househusband: he made good soup, welcomed the kids home for lunch, signed their notes, rallied for after-school crises. On the other hand, I knew an artist with a studio in his garden who treated his work like a nine-to-five job and walked away from the household and child-care responsibilities. He is divorced now and I'm not sure it's because one of his models was too attractive to resist or because his wife started to paint too. I knew a divorced writer who farmed out his children and obligations to whichever wife was the mother responsible. Older now – so are his kids – he is providing a home in return for their housekeeping duties.

Lots of men cook now, but most of them still forget the vegetables. They also seem to have a higher tolerance for dirt though a lot of them like things to be neat. They spend more time than their fathers did playing with their children but they still aren't very good about interruptions or cleanup. Most of them are happy to have their wives work when it comes to spending that second paycheck but they still aren't willing to spend as much time on the housework to help her. The key word is *help*, instead of *share*. Housework and child care are still considered the wife's (almost) sole responsibility, whether or not she works outside the home. She remains the harassed center at mission control, working double time, trying to find more energy and hours in a day that has only 24 hours in it.

Children can't be expected to wait until there's more time, forced into a neat corner until it's convenient to deal with them. All the efficiency in the world won't replace TLC. The good news is that it's comforting to be with loved ones. The bad news is that without it, without the time and attention they need, kids will find a replacement, not always a good one.

Most women's magazines still offer cookies and advice and lots of tips on how to juggle home, children and job. In my day, I studied *Management in the Home*, efficiency expert Lillian Gilbreth's advice on time-management in the home, mainly because I wanted to release some time and energy to write. I remember a friend who called on me, saw my notes and asked what I was doing. When I explained, she said in disbelief, "You mean you're using your free time to find out how to release more free time?"

Yes. It's all we have, any of us – 24 hours a day – and we must use that time well.

THE STAY-AT-HOME MOTHER

It is impossible for any woman to love her children
twenty-four hours a day.
– Milton R. Sapirstein

Work outside the home now is not only necessary and accepted for most women, it is also expected. A woman, on meeting another woman, asks "What do you do?" and she doesn't expect to hear about Home and School or pickling. Every woman does that in her spare (hah!) time.

Whereas in the 1950s the woman who worked was looked down on for neglecting her husband, children, and home, the woman in the 1980s was regarded as a sloven and a parasite if she stayed home and looked after the children while her husband did all the work(!). At the same time, women who were trying to do it all kept reminding their husbands that housework didn't get done all by itself and children couldn't be put on hold like a demanding client.

Now, in the 1990s, though a working women's salary is considered a necessary part of the family income, some mothers are making a conscious choice to stay home and "bond" with the kids – for a while, anyway. It's a difficult decision because it's costly, not only because of the actual income forfeited but also because of the interest lost on her Retirement Savings Plan, which she cannot contribute to unless she has earned income or her husband opts for a Spousal Plan. Even if her work outside the home doesn't amount to a career which she has interrupted, she still may have lost some accrual of company benefits or pension. Still, tight as it is trying to get along on one income, most stay-at-home mothers feel it's worth it. They're rare, though, not only in attitude but in numbers, part of that 4 percent who make up the nuclear family, giving their children what they had: cookies after school and someone there to listen. Maybe that's what husbands really want, too.

Polls indicate that while most young men expect their wives to work, and welcome the money coming in, they still want all their creature comforts, the cookies and the hand-ironed shirts. (I knew women who *ironed* Perma-Press to please their husbands; I even knew a woman who ironed diapers!) Catch-22. "Just a housewife" may be easy to put down, but it hurts to lose her services.

Housewife, by the way, is no longer a valid description, and has been eliminated from the Canadian census, thanks to a New Zealand professor of social policy, Marilyn Waring, who wrote a wonderful, subversive book *If Women Counted: A New Feminist Economics*, in which she argued that women's work should be taken into account in the estimates of a country's Gross National Product. She believes that the census is one of the basic tools governments use to keep women invisible.

In 1991, Carol Lees, a Saskatchewan woman, refused to answer the question on her census form that asked how many hours she had worked in the last week, "not including volunteer work, housework, [home] maintenance or repairs." That was all she had done – for 19 years at home with three children, and she was "mighty annoyed!"

Refusing to answer a census is illegal in Canada and Lees faced prosecution. Never an activist before, she began a protest campaign, forming a support group (the Canadian Alliance for Home Managers), proposing to boycott the next census if unpaid work remained uncounted. In 1996, Lee's lobbying paid off, given a boost a year earlier when the National Action Committee on the Status of Women (NAC) endorsed her cause. Canada was one of the first, if not the first, countries in the world to count the hours spent performing housework and child care without pay. The May 1996 census included questions on unpaid labor; the household activities section was divided into three parts: house or yard work, child care, and senior care.

It's uphill work – not the labor, but changing men's minds. The dollar value of women's services still remains too low, mostly because so much of it has been discounted. Why pay a child-care worker much when mothers do it for free? A corollary of this question used to be held up to daughters when their mothers warned them to hang on to their virginity until marriage: "Why buy a cow when you can get the milk for free?"

"Women's work" has yet to be computed, and it's not only the work women do in the home. The labor that North American farm wives contribute and the unpaid work that women do in subsistence economies (walking for water, growing food) to keep their families alive is going to have to be recognized. At the United Nations Fourth World Conference on Women held in Beijing in 1995 the final document, a "Platform for Action," calls for nations to begin an assessment of the value of unpaid work.

Canada's first woman elected to the House of Commons, Agnes MacPhail, was also among the first to try to estimate the value of women's services. By this time, we've all seen the lists: so much per hour for laundry and cleaning services, cooking, chauffeuring, baby-sitting, and so on. So far no one has managed to put a price on mental anguish. Jessie Bernard called the emotional work of women in the home *motherwork*. Feminist writer Gloria Steinem calls the physical work in the home *shitwork*. At any rate, the jobs keep multiplying along with their estimated market price and women remain unpaid for their work at home.

Whenever it is suggested that the ones who didn't work outside the home receive a government pension for their work at retirement age, the protest is that women who work outside also do the home work and yet they would receive only their earned pension. Another Catch-22. As for the quality of the work, since there is as yet no remuneration there are no evaluations or prizes, so the idea has never arisen that messier homes or indifferent cooking deserve less reward than Good Housekeeping perfection. At least a woman can be comforted by the fact that her mate is no longer "head of the house" on the census, but merely, "householder." It's a beginning.

By staying at home a mother eases both that terrible guilt she feels every day about neglecting her children and the bone-weariness of trying to handle two (or more) jobs. American feminist writer Tillie Olsen suggests both painful aspects in her classic award-winning story, "I Stand Here Ironing":

> *I did not know then what I know now – the fatigue of the long day, and the lacerations of group life in nurseries that are only parking places for children.*

It's hard to juggle one child, husband and job, but it can be done and made to look easy. With two or more children it gets tougher. Time, time is the killer. There's never enough of it, never enough to go around, to get everything done, keep everyone happy, and still get enough rest to do a good job. So it is increasingly tempting to take some "time off," be a full-time mother, give the children a good start. Women are consciously making this choice now, not in huge numbers, but in numbers large enough to constitute a vanguard, a trend that may develop. Or not.

On my television show *Women, Lifestyle and Money*, in the episode on Stay-at-Home Mothers, I interviewed a couple of contemporary young mothers who had made the choice to stay at home. One, happy at a mature age to be bonding with her first baby, is still ecstatic but also realistic and fully expects to pick up her career when she weans her little girl. The other one has found staying home so satisfying that after six years at home with her child who is now ready to enter school, she is reluctant to return to the work force. Besides, she argues, she's rusty, having lost too much knowledge to be able to step back in easily.

One detects in her argument the beginning of another kind of desperation: a feeling of being left behind, a sense of isolation. I hear echoes of the 1950s mother mustering all the strength of her pent-up intelligence to cope with the little minds in her care plus all the mindless, repetitive home duties that could, if one were working on the outside, either be justifiably disregarded or left to the not-so-thorough attentions of a hired cleaner. The biggest problem stay-at-home mothers have this time round is that they haven't any company. They are too scattered and isolated to do each other any good.

"I may be home," one told me, "but my next-door neighbor isn't." Neither are her neighbor's kids. Playmates are in short supply because the kids next door are in day care. If a SAH (stay-at-home) needs back-up care in case of an emergency, she'll have to call 911.

I have met a few stay-at-home mothers who sell their home time, providing day care for one or two children about the same age as their own. What I and my contemporaries used to do on a part-time basis as favors or barter has turned into yet another cottage industry.

Even for those mothers who don't turn a penny on home care – and even more for those who do – loneliness and the burden of full responsibility can weigh heavy. One women's advisor suggests that SAHs regard their home time not as a step backward or sideways, but as a positive move. They can, she says, prepare for re-entry to the business world. The trouble with that idea, argues one of my mothers, is that there is no time for uninterrupted, focused study. She's lucky if she manages to read a couple of pages in a novel before she falls asleep.

Most women do return to full-time work when the children are older. Stats Can reminds us that women, like their men folk, will be spending about 45 years of their lives in the labor force. These stay-at-home years are for most women merely an interim, albeit a costly one. Financial sacrifice is involved, although it is balanced to some extent by the savings: no child-care expenses; fewer, less expensive clothes; perhaps only one car; lower food costs (frugal shopping and cooking takes time). One young woman who tried it both ways went back to work in spite of the higher costs, spending most of her salary on child care. She sums up the hidden costs for a lot of women: "I went stir-crazy. Here at work I feel fulfilled."

It has to do with perception, one's own and others' perception of one's worth. When nations – read "male-dominated governments" – really begin to count the contribution to the GNP that stay-at-home women make, and the enormous value of it, then the prize will seem worth the cost.

Does anyone even remember the novel *Diary of a Mad Housewife* by Sue Kaufman? She was describing my generation. We were indeed mad, ripe for rebellion when Betty Friedan published *The Feminine Mystique* in 1963. For some of my peers it was too late to change. Change would have made a mockery of what they had invested their lives in. Their/my children have grown up now, so they/I are not insane any more – no more than is normal. But some of them are angry because they have become victims of the mid-life dump. That's another story. And some of them are vaguely dissatisfied, wondering if they missed something. The Big Generation we spawned has different problems, not the least of which is money.

ATTITUDES TO MONEY

One of the pleasantest things in married life
is that you have no money of your own,
but have to come to your husband for every sixpence.
– M.V. Hughes, *A London Girl of the 1880s*

The family, we seldom stop to realize, is one of the major economic units of society today. It's no longer the major producing unit, but it is still a consuming unit. Although families no longer provide the goods and services by which each one functions, they still need them: birthing and child care; the preparation of food, brewing and preserving; the production of cloth and the manufacture and cleaning of clothes; education; care of the sick and the dying; the laying-out of the dead. Most of these used to be women's tasks and most of them have been taken outside the home and put into the hands of professionals, that is, people who get paid for their services.

The family still controls the reproduction of human beings, despite the efforts of test-tube fathers and scientists with a petri dish. It still provides the first training in language and cultural behavior, as well as basic education and life skills. The family is the moral and social arbiter of a nation and also the psychological barometer. Being the foundation upon which we build everything else, that is, public appearance, performance, lifestyle, culture, morality, and values, the family's role is beneath conscious recognition most of the time. It is also beyond price.

That doesn't stop some people from trying to put a price tag on it, not only the cost of the services homemakers provide – and her services keep going up in estimate if not in estimation – but also the cost of rearing a child. The Vanier Institute of the Family, as already noted, now pegs the price of a no-frills child from birth to age 18 at $150,000 – so that doesn't include the cost of post-secondary education. The question is, is it worth it?

Of course it's not, if we insist on putting price tags on people. Price-tag mentalities are not new, but they're still scary, especially when applied to human values, which can't be bought though they can be paid for. The family is still our main life-support system, and it costs more than money to maintain.

Surveys (will they never end?) reveal that people without children can offer at least eight good reasons why they don't have them, and they say they're happier. (Compared to what? How can they tell?) People with children can't think of one good logical reason for having them – yet they go on rearing them and loving them. Where would any of us be without them? Soon dead and forever gone.

Just as important as the price of kids and the economic worth of a wife are the values of the family itself. People seem to have no qualms about premarital sex, but they very seldom get intimate about money before marriage. Those who live together common law, an arrangement increasing in frequency in recent years, may share a bed and rent but keep separate bank accounts. Some may opt for a contract, allowing for a fair distribution of goods in the case of a breakup, but they often keep their private ambitions and desires secret. To many couples, marriage presents revelations – financial, not sexual.

Again, advice abounds. Most magazines now offer a regular money column; banks and trust and insurance companies provide brochures with budgets and lists with blanks to fill in with details of ownership, income, outgo, insurance, wills, and so on. Most of the questions are not difficult; gathering the answers is kind of fun, sort of like a scavenger hunt. People love to feel as if they're getting organized.

Much more difficult to sort out and recognize are *attitudes* toward money and *behavior* – the handling of money – not always the same thing. A new husband will discover strange tendencies in a woman he thought he knew; a wife will discover controlling aspects in him she hadn't guessed. They find that though they may be willing to share a toothbrush in a pinch, they are more reluctant to pool their resources. A couple may find that although they may agree that they are determined to save money – for a cruise, a car, a house, retirement, whatever – one half of the pair keeps sabotaging most of their good intentions with little treats and extravagances or sometimes big ones that dissipate their savings.

Money books abound, full of sensible advice, but a mate's unexpected behavior can become a booby trap without any warning. Games might help.

Games are gratuitous and they're supposed to be fun. I remember years ago playing *Probe* with friends. It's a word association game. One of the wives in our group, when presented with the word *love*, answered instantly without thinking, which is what you're supposed to do.

"Money!" she shouted, and we all looked at her husband with new eyes.

Another game, *Scruples*, enables people to play with ideas and check out attitudes painlessly, that is, without it costing an arm and a leg. Even better but more time-consuming than a game is *The Book of Questions* by Gregory Stock, designed to stimulate a lively conversation (to say the least!). It can also reveal information not easily discovered, and not only about money. Here are a few sample questions about the material world:

> *Would you accept $1,000,000 to leave the country and never set foot in it again?*

> *If you knew of a way to use your estate, following your death, to greatly benefit humanity, would you do it and leave only a minimal amount to your family?*

> *For $20,000 would you go for three months without washing, brushing your teeth, or using deodorant? Assume you could not explain your reasons to anyone, and that there would be no long-term effect on your career.*

> *Knowing you have a 50 percent chance of winning and would be paid 10 times the amount of your bet if you won, what fraction of what you now own would you be willing to wager?*

Discussions like this can cause loud disagreement, but better in the abstract than in real life.

Double-income families are the ones that have rendered the nuclear family almost obsolete by putting the wife to work outside the home. Apart from the logistics of it – the handling of time, the juggling of tasks and children, coping with stress, all that – one of the major considerations is money, and this should be discussed (and regularly reviewed). First of all, of course, the question arises: is the money coming in adequate compensation for the high cost of making it? But second, and just as important, is where does the money go? Do both incomes go into one pot? Is there an agreement as to who pays for what? In the event of a divorce, who gets what, and is the division fair? Is it clear why the highest income should cover the big expenses (in order to lower the tax on it) so that no residual resentment is going to cause a quarrel? No one – least of all husbands and wives – can afford to be naive or dewy-eyed about money.

There are still wives who have no discretionary money of their own, who have no sense of money, though they may be whizzes with the household accounts and great shoppers for sales. They still are, as the National Council of Women puts it, "one man away from welfare." What they could use is *Everywoman's Money Book*, by Lynne Macfarlane and me, to help them with the basics: getting credit in their own name, income splitting, effective saving, and so on. That involves a little practical – but constant – effort.

What I'm concerned with here is attitudes. It has been noted, and not only by me, that when both parents work, the one with the lower income is usually the one on deck in the event of an emergency: child's illness, an aging parent's problem (no matter whose parent), special event, whatever. Since women earn at best only 70 percent of what men earn (for full-time work in certain professions; most women still earn about 60 percent of men's salaries), the wife/mother is usually the one on call. In the case of any decision involving a certain amount of sacrifice of time or effort, the nasty question often arises: how much are her services and time worth? We've already had that discussion.

It has also been noted that a woman's chance of divorce increases with every $1000 a month she earns. This is not the threat to uppity women that it might appear. The statistics don't say which spouse opts out; more frequently at higher levels of salary, it's the woman, because she has the financial ability to do so. Even so, it's a step she should consider carefully because women's incomes usually go down drastically after a divorce while men's go up.

It's important for both parties to determine their attitude to money and to its source. The designations *Yours*, *Mine* and *Ours* are not as simply defined as they seem, especially when one or the other half of the couple is hanging onto something with both hands clenched tight. Some working wives who used to stay home figure now that what's yours is mine and what's mine is also mine. On the other hand, some husbands figure that what's mine is mine and what you make is also mine – and that, in fact, is the way it used to be when women were not allowed to own property in their own names. The question now is who owns what, if anything, and what are they going to do with it?

I talk to a lot of people about money, and I find people's attitudes to it fascinating. Sometimes I think I should pay them! One woman came up to me after a talk I gave and challenged me.

"You say save 10 percent of your income," she accused. I nodded; she'd listened. "My husband used to make us save 90 and live on 10," she said. "He's dead now and I'm having the best time!"

Earlier than that, I was talking to a group of women about insurance, mentioning the need of a little disability insurance for wives in case of an illness. I asked who would look after the children? (I've seen statistics revealing that a wife's long-term illness can cost a family's savings in attempts to replace her services.) A woman put up her hand (it was a large group) and told us, "My husband says he doesn't need to insure me because I'm not worth anything." She had more at risk than disability.

Another woman I know, with a lucrative business of her own, stopped the life insurance salesman as he was closing his books after selling her husband a new policy. "What about me?" she asked.

What about me? Yes, indeed, but *what about us?*

People keep on making choices. Not as many are choosing children as used to. Quite a few who have children thrust upon them, as it were, are choosing negatively before (abortion) or after (divorce and custody given to the other parent) the fact. The birth rate is dropping, almost below-zero growth, so that we will as a country be relying on the influx of immigrants to keep growing. With dwindling numbers and an increasing aging population, we will be facing further economic effects – depressing ones.

Growth and production are arguably dependent on a consuming home market. If the home market declines, then so does the entire economy. People start, have started, saving for a rainy day, causing rainy days to come sooner. Even divorce, a growth industry, producing two households where there was one and which therefore requires duplication of equipment – beds, stoves, dishes, TVs and so on – won't help much.

Everything gets political these days. Suddenly finances become a politically charged subject – for the nation as well as for the family. Does anyone care?

8

TLC

Govern a family as you would cook a small fish
– very gently.
– Chinese proverb

COMMUNICATION

This is not a how-to book. I have no intention of telling anyone how to rear a child. Mature as I am, I'm simply not qualified. Old as I am, all I can report is what I have seen. I won't tell anyone either to do as I have done or do as I say. In any case, advice abounds: entire magazines and books and college courses are devoted to parents, mothers, children, families and their relationships, education, health. Family therapy is a growth industry, and doesn't need me to water it. What I can do is discuss and conjecture, maybe start a conversation, fan a spark of recognition, give a little twist to a curl of thought. It's called communication, and that's what families (should) do best.

Communication: 1. the act or fact of passing along;
transmitting. 2. a giving or exchanging of information by
talking, writing, etc.
– Gage Canadian Dictionary

Communication begins with talking, but doesn't end there. It's a place to start. Communication skills are among the most important tools a person can have in business these days. Every company with a message provides seminars and workshops for its employees to learn these skills and pays huge sums of money to consultants who are experts not only at communication but also at communicating the skills of communicating. Families could use such an expert. Communicating is one of the most essential acts a family performs both within its membership and then outside, for it is within the family unit that an individual first learns how to interact with others.

Here's one of the questions that rises: what happens to this resource and how is the skill developed, when families are so small as to eliminate communication skills? Where will people learn to communicate and negotiate? Cooperation begins with two; so do generosity, sympathy, empathy and compromise. Well, all it takes is two. Two plus time.

Time, like many things, is best when it's shared. Taking time is a conscious act and demonstrates very clearly where interest and genuine concern lie. "Parents can give things to their children or they can spend time with their children," wrote Matthew Addison,* when he was a little boy in the third grade in Nederland, Texas. "Time is best." Time is a clear form of communication, generous allotments of it. One-minute management may be effective in an office; one-minute parenting doesn't work. Time with children should be regular, by appointment, as well as spontaneous, but written in stone – anticipated and graciously given, along with undivided attention.

That means listening. Lots of parents lecture their kids when they think they're talking to them and end by saying something like "I'm

---

* quoted in *Children's Rules for Parents: Wit and Wisdom from Schoolchildren Around the Country*, gathered by Michael Laser and Ken Goldner. Perennial Library, Harper & Row, New York, 1987

glad we had this little chat." Uh huh. Even when they're supposed to be listening, grownups don't always hear what is being said, or if they do hear, they leap to conclusions, pass judgments, encourage half-truths and fudging, not to say outright lies. Or they correct the kid's grammar, interrupt to remind her to call her grandmother, to tell him to clip his nails or to stop biting them, and then wonder why the conversation stops.

It's important to listen to what family members are not saying as well as to what they're talking about. Fear of ridicule or judgment, embarrassment or shyness, or a reticence to show emotion can all deflect truth, or mask it. It's easy to be detached about strangers and others – coworkers, neighbors and so on – but it's difficult, given one's own emotional involvement, to listen to one's family, especially when it's so hard to talk back. In his book *Knots*, R. D. Laing presents a dilemma that expresses some of this:

> *Jack can't tell Jill what he wants Jill to tell him.*
> *Jill can't tell him either because although Jill knows X*
> *Jill does not know that Jack does not know X.*

We all withhold evidence, and that complicates things, causing what Susan Griffin calls a "chain reaction of silences." It is important to share information, but to do that one must have trust. Sharing ideas, thoughts, plans, and to a certain extent, worries – but not more than the child can bear – is a good idea whose time has passed and should come again. One of the advantages the children of single parents have over children of intact families is that they get more of that one parent's attention and share more of her thoughts (sometimes too much!). Children, especially maturing adolescents, can be among a single parent's best friends (or worst enemies!). Single parents not only allow their children into their lives, they need them. As a result, they have to be careful not to dump on them.

THE FAMILY AT TABLE

The metaphor for the planetary community, to replace the
old image of men on horseback riding around the planet
keeping us all in order, may be that of the family at the
dinner table: the world family at the world dinner table.
The family at the table is a basic human metaphor of
sharing.

– Elise Boulding

The double-income family has caused the biggest change in family eating patterns in this century – that, and television. A glance at the TV
commercials shows us what people are eating and why. Speed, convenience and other pressures make for fast food, take-out, pickup meals, and
scattered consumers. That's what the food purveyors would have us believe. So what's on the menu, besides junk food?

Junk food used to have nothing to do with the family at table. It is the
enemy of quality and nutrition and family unity. It increases the number
of "food contacts," as the food experts call them, to about 20 per day, as
opposed to the old-time three squares. Families don't eat together
anymore; they graze. Breakfast, if taken, is solitary, standing up and being sure to wash the bowl and spoon (cereal), or plate and knife (toasted
bagel and cream cheese). The midday meal is the same: a sandwich in
the hand is cheaper than a Big Mac at the corner, and no one is at home.
Dinner is often eaten on the run, en route to somewhere. Perhaps this is
the reason so many families eat an estimated three dinners at home a
week. So the cook(s) rely on the freezer, the microwave and the take-
out – convenience, processed food.

Breaking bread together – or pita, pizzas, tacos, tortillas – is a
wonderfully intimate human act and should be cherished. Nourish-

ment begins at the table but does not end there; it goes on to nurturance (Boulding's word), nowhere more evident than when a parent is feeding its young. It used to be considered a solely female task, because we have mistakenly assigned it exclusively to women in the past. Granted, the preparation and serving of food are complex acts, and they depend upon enough money to buy the raw material. Divorced men find it one of the biggest challenges of single fatherhood – the preparation, that is. Single mothers usually find the challenge begins earlier – at the market, in the pocketbook.

But the family at table, this is what family is all about, not the food (though it's important). It's about the opportunity to eat together, and to share news, hopes, disappointments, to solve each other's problems, to listen, to communicate – hey, to laugh! Family is more than a bunch of statistics; family is human beings in action. Where better to see them in action than at table? What do we see? What do we learn?

RULES AND MANNERS

- Don't lean the side of your arm on the table.
- Don't talk with your mouth full.
- Stop poking your sister with your fork.
- No phone calls or TV during meals.
- Don't shovel your food in without chewing.
- Stop kicking your brother.
- You eat like a pig.
- How many times have I told you to ask, not stretch?
- Please pass the salt (easy on the sodium); butter (watch out for cholesterol); bread (make sure it's whole-grain).
- Don't tease the baby.

TABLE CONVERSATION

➤ So what did you do at school today? (Interrogation as an attempt at companionship.)

➤ You did what???

➤ A funny thing happened on my way to the office...

➤ Can I have the car on Saturday night?

➤ Is that really dead cow/pig/chicken? (fledgling vegetarian)

➤ I'm just not hungry.

➤ We will now discuss a) junk food, b) eating between meals, c) anorexia nervosa.

GENDER ROLES AND THE FAMILY

➤ Why do I always have to clean up and never him?

➤ Listen to your father.

➤ Don't be rude to your mother.

➤ Sit still, I'll get the coffee. (Who said that?)

I will never forget the night of the Great Brussels Sprouts Mutiny. Our children put their forks and their feet down simultaneously and refused ever to eat brussels sprouts again, and my husband and I agreed with them. Never had we experienced such unanimity as a family! The kids tried it again a few weeks later with another kind of sprouts (bean) but I reserved some rights. Thin ends of the wedge, or sprouts, as the case may be, could in time lead to boycotting of an entire food class, if one is not careful. The point is that the dinner table is almost the only place where the entire family is sometimes in agreement.

Just as we function on automatic pilot with leftover commands from our childhood, so we respond to familiar food and situations. At its simplest, the most comforting food of our childhood was usually heavy on the carbohydrate, but quite bland, milky, or eggy, salty or sweet about equally divided. A friend of mine keeps having me for dinner and serving me his favorite comfort food: macaroni and cheese, with applesauce and brussels sprouts – I still haven't told him how I feel about those sprouts. I eat one, for manners – something else one picks up at an early age in a family.

Comfort food possesses therapeutic, almost magical qualities for the layered memories it evokes: a wonderful, wet, stay-at-home cold when Mom (or someone) brought hot lemon and honey or chicken soup; a pot of chili after a sleigh ride; cold chicken and potato salad on a picnic; Thanksgiving or Christmas or Hanukkah when food and family were part of a precious ritual. The feasts of the past telescope into one long dinner, beautifully set and lighted, with the food always hot and delicious and with members of the family entering and leaving as they pass through our lives. How blessed are we if we have a Long Dinner like that tucked away in memory. Many, of course, do not.

What a contrast those ritual feasts present to junk food. To many kids – and some adults – junk food is what couch potatoes love best: lebenty-seven different flavors, cuts, thicknesses and shapes of potato chips, fried or baked, high- or low-fat (and don't mention olestra yet); five varieties of pretzels; multiflavored popcorn with butter flavor, air-popped or in microwave packages; white bread slathered with hydrogenated peanut butter; nachos with or without refried beans but always with cheese and salsa (actually, not bad nutritionally but a killer for fat); sugar-coated cereal; and any drink that ends in -"ade" and doesn't have nerdies in it. (Some food manufacturers add lumps to fruit-flavored drinks to give them "mouth feel.")

Early feminist Charlotte Perkins Gilman in her book *Women and Economics* (1898) commented that "a family unity which is only bound together with a tablecloth is of questionable value." These days we're lucky if we get place mats, but there's no doubt about the value of the dinner table. It's one of the places where family unity begins.

Rituals

You don't start traditions, traditions start.
– Skinnell's Rule

Every family knows about rituals. Rituals are why airlines make money and people go broke getting home for the holidays, attending family weddings, baptisms, bar and bat mitzvahs, anniversaries and funerals. Rituals illustrate better than anything exactly what a functioning family is all about: growth, process, change; memory, loyalty, solidarity. They provide what Robert Glossop calls *lines of demarcation* by which we can measure and observe growth and change, taking due note, acknowledging the passage of time. I call it door-frame reckoning.

Gifts shops now sell fancy, long fold-out paper charts decorated with Winnie the Pooh or some kitschy anthropomorphic animal, with the years printed on the side of a measurement chart so parents can mark and see how much little Billy has grown. In my day we used a door frame. Every summer, when we went back to our cottage at the lake, we would back up against the pencil marks on the door frame to see how much we had grown in a year. Now I do it for my grandchildren – one door frame to a family – every year when they visit. That's a line of demarcation. It gives us all a nice sense of continuity, no matter how much else changes over the year. That's what ritual is about.

It's all too easy to reduce ritual to worn-out traditions and cheap sentiment but sometimes difficult to distinguish between them. Whether deeply religious or borderline pagan, most North American families celebrate annual events with a lot of help from Hallmark. The cards and gift wrap – and the gifts! – go along with the candles, songs, food, and sometimes even worship. (It's getting so the churches, synagogues and temples are almost empty except at festival times.) As procreative families are formed, they absorb and assimilate – or reject – the traditions of their families of origin and create new traditions and rituals of their own. I've been watching my children do this as they struggle with complications I never encountered: divorce, custody, more in-laws than you can shake a stick at. It's fascinating to see new rituals being formed and old rituals being adapted and changed, and comforting too, because of the semblance of unity and normality they impart.

Best-selling pop psychologist Wayne Dyer (*Your Erroneous Zones*, *Pulling Your Own Strings*, etc.) endeared himself to the Me Decade of the 1980s by telling people they didn't have to dance to others' tunes. He said no one had to be subject to the family's "roll call." If a fellow would rather be in Florida at Christmas than with his preachy parents, snotty sister and boozy brother, he could just take off. Dyer must have been talking about divorced men without custody. Nothing is going to stop such a selfish person – except maybe a very dormant conscience. There is still something like a sense of obligation within families, thank goodness.

What's wrong with roll call? There are times when other people really are more important than Number One, and ritual family times are most of them. That's why airlines will never go broke at Thanksgiving or Christmas. It's not the getaway trips to Florida that are keeping the planes in the sky. It's families.

As for the rest of the calendar year, the card companies would also go broke if we didn't have such a pathological love of ritual, honoring as we do everything from babies to graduation to weddings, anniversaries and funerals and all the birthdays in between. People don't write letters these days, though they do send faxes and e-mail. They still send cards because a witty remark is as good as a thousand words.

There are times, however, when gestures transcend words and turn into rituals which in turn transcend time and distill love. A private ritual, layered with memory, becomes a symbol of a relationship, an era, a family in time.

My father was a very ritualistic man; some of his rituals live on in several of my procreative families. I will add to this list others that I have picked up from Open Line Shows across the country, when people reported to me their favorite family rituals.

PRIVATE RITUALS

‣ Happy First of the Month. Not just Happy New Year, but Happy New Month. There's a game involved as well: first one to remember what day it is and to wish the others Happy First-of-Whatever wins. The prize is its own reward. Larks tend to win over nightingales in this ritual but it's surprising how many hours of a day can pass before someone remembers it's the first of the month. Some families say "Rabbits" just for fun; others wait and celebrate the second day of the month. I know a couple of families, including mine, who have a member with a birthday on the 13th of the month, so 13 is lucky and celebrated, even Friday the 13th.

‣ Birthday Parade. The person whose birthday it is stays in bed, pretending to sleep. The other members of the family get up a little earlier, gather together and parade in to the Birthday Person singing the birthday song and bearing loot. To wake up like that once a year, convinced that you are the most important person in the world and that your presence means a lot to other people, is a wonderful feeling. In the case of small families, one has to use some ingenuity to make a parade. When I moved into Toronto with the boys after my husband died, Liz and Kate both showed up at 7 a.m. for John's first birthday in the new place, Liz from residence at York University on the outskirts of the city and Kate from residence in Wilfrid Laurier University at Waterloo, 60 miles away, and neither of them had a car. Ah, the power of ritual!

‣ TLs. Does anyone else know about Trade-Lasts? A Trade-Last is something nice someone else said about a member of the family, offered to that person *after* he or she remembers something nice a third party said about the trader. The other-party compliment is traded *last*. There's always an account owing on one side or the other, but someone usually remembers who owes whom. It can be played with friends but it's better in the family because everyone shares in it.

➤ Pudding Stories. This was one of my rituals. When we went on long car trips (in the early days a long car trip was the hour and a half it took us to drive to the lake), I used to tell my children Pudding Stories. Each child was allowed to give me one "ingredient" and I'd make up a story using them all. Good training for a writer and good entertainment for the kids. My son tells Pudding Stories to his children. I know a family with an only child that allows the child three ingredients, at intervals.

➤ And then there are pumpkins to carve, Hamentashen to bake, Easter eggs to color, cinnamon hearts to stir in the applesauce, and marshmallows to toast over the fall bonfire or on the barbecue, and all those familiar activities repeated every year that no one thinks of as rituals, but they are.

➤ One of my informants remembered fall apples and her father paring one carefully for each of the kids while they watched an unbroken peel fall away from his knife – and then the game of finding out her future mate by tossing the peel over her shoulder and reading the letter it formed.

➤ Another remembered her father examining her school books each fall and carefully signing her name in each one with his fountain pen (in the days when textbooks were bought not borrowed).

➤ No one I know pipes in a haggis but just about every meat-eater who can afford it carries the festive roast in to the family table with some flourish.

➤ The most common ritual, scarcely considered a ritual now, is Sunday brunch, before, after or instead of church. Post-church brunches often start with Mimosa (equal parts champagne and fresh-squeezed orange juice) but pre-church Cappuccino is good too. Even men who do no other cooking will prepare breakfast on Sunday, and each has his specialty. I know one man who cooks sourdough pancakes for his family on Sunday morning and another who makes the most exquisite, delicate crêpes, and another who makes marvelous (fattening) home fries.

➤ Storying. This is a useful ritual my father began. I still do it for myself, privately. Sociologist Boulding recommends it.

Here's how storying worked for me. At the end of some event – it could be the end of each day on a car trip, or the end of summer holidays, or the end of exams, or of a school election (I lost), or later, the end of a college romance – my father would say, "Let's summarize what happened and what we/you accomplished." Then he'd go on to point out that we had driven 500 miles and crossed three state lines, or that I had earned a swimming badge, or passed another milestone on the highway of life (people used to say things like that in those days, not just my father), or that I'd learned a lot from that boy – and my father seemed to know how much! And I'd nod and say, "Yes, yes, that's how it was," and it was as if he had given me my experience to hold and keep forever.

He did the same when he was dying (of cancer of the liver). The terminal illness was brief, as illnesses go, but it gave my father enough time to summarize his life, as if to say, "This is what I learned, and this is what dying is like." I listened and I nodded. "Yes, yes, that's how it was." I later learned that the final, major step in coming to terms with death is that kind of acceptance.

So was that ritual or therapy?

What I'm really talking about is *history*. All these rituals, traditions and memories create a living, changing history of each family as it grows and interacts and keeps on changing. The family is dynamic, an organism with a collective life of its own, separate and individual and unique unto itself, a sum of all its parts. That, of course, is why divorce can never be completely final, because memory can't be wiped out and history doesn't cease to exist. Each family's traditions and rituals help to identify it and help it, also, to keep on growing, to add cumulative layers, like rings on a tree.

Birth and death, with confirmations and bar and bat mitzvahs and rites of passage and weddings (and divorces) in between – that's what family history is about, on and on and on, and if it isn't forever, it begins to look like it. Looking at pictures in a family album, hanging the ornaments on a tree, telling stories, both real and made-up, remembering family jokes – all these simple activities give us a handle on our family and ultimately, ideally, on our own place in society and in history.

Sometimes, however, something is withheld. A secret can be benign; more often it is malignant and can damage a family with unspoken fear or erode it with a hidden cancer.

SECRETS

If I tell here all the secrets that I know,
public and private,
perhaps I will be able to see the way the old sometimes see.
– Susan Griffin

In her book *A Chorus of Stones* Susan Griffin describes a secret in her own family that she didn't discover until she was well into adulthood.

She says that everything she was taught at home and school was "colored by denial," so familiar that she didn't see it. It had to do with the transgression of her grandmother and her erasure from the family. Vague about the details, Griffin concluded that her grandmother left her family for another man, causing her husband and mother-in-law to abandon her in Canada and move with her two sons to California. No one was allowed to grieve, but the loss of her haunted the family.

Griffin's book assesses the damage this kind of secret wreaks, both privately and publicly. Apart from the actual event that is hidden, a feeling is also secreted, and it does not disappear. Pain is denied because the source of pain is denied, and does worse harm than if acknowledged. The body, writes Griffin, "takes up the rage, the pain, the disowned memory."

It's a freak of synchronicity, as Jung called it, when two related events happen though far apart, or when a new idea recurs several times within a short time span. This kind of recurrence happened to me when I was first beginning to think about family secrets. Within the time frame of one month, I heard of three of them, told me all unbidden and unexpected by chance acquaintances on a plane, at a dinner, taking a course with strangers. Here is the secret: that one of the children in an unsplit family was not the child of both parents.

In one case, that of a young woman, she didn't find out until she was grown and too alienated from her mother to wonder any more why she had been denied all her life. Still smarting from the recent knowledge, she told me that she was her mother's child – among six siblings, older and younger – from a hopeless love affair during a long absence of the husband. Her mother went away for a while and came back with a story and a "friend's child" whom she had decided to adopt. The mother never acknowledged her natural daughter to her older daughters until a year or so before her death, and never at all to the girl herself. Yet the secret hung in the family air, permeating the atmosphere, scenting all their relationships. The "adopted" daughter has become a writer, with something to expiate.

A man on a plane told me he was the middle child of five by his father, but that he was the product of his father's affair with another woman. His father's wife – incredible woman! – took him in and raised him with her own. I got the impression that this man's origins became an open secret within the family. Remember Gloucester's legitimate and illegitimate sons in *King Lear* and the way he acknowledged Edmund's parentage?

> *His breeding, sir, hath been at my charge...*
>
> *there was good sport at his making,*
>
> *and the whoreson must be acknowledged.*

Shakespeare never was one to mince words.

My seat companion never married, he told me, but keeps "friends" – not even Significant Others – in different cities, sort of like the captain in that old movie *Captain's Paradise*, a ferry boat captain who had a wife and family in his two ports of call. I've seen a remake of the idea on a Sunday Night Movie, only the captain was an airline pilot.

A married woman told me of an affair she had that resulted in a child who her husband, knowing of her lapse, acknowledged as his own, and they were very close. This was a well kept secret. The two other daughters waited a long time before they had children but remained unmarried; the oldest son married and divorced, childless, and has deep-seated problems with his relationships. The putative father died and the girl never did know. She married a man old enough to be her father. Are these people all a product, all-unknowing, of the secret?

R. D. Laing pointed out that every family has secrets, and that whatever our entry point, we have to play out the drama we are born into. "But there are plays within plays within plays," he says. The question is, where does keeping a secret leave off and withholding damaging evidence cut in?

I have already quoted Erving Goffman who also believes that every family has its secrets but he approves of their being kept – some of them. Some benign secrets are tacit but open, unspoken perhaps but expected, based on an almost automatic habit of denial, like white lies. Others, more serious and closely guarded, form part of the foundation of the family, a foundation with serious cracks, whose discovery may crumble the entire structure.

It's modern lore now that adoptive children should be told the facts of their birth and be allowed to seek out their biological parents. Kids today aren't granted any delicious paranoid speculation about whether they're adopted and if that's why their parents are so nasty to them. People are so hygienic in their mind-sets these days that the adoption data are no longer secret, they're open, part of a case history. The adult children's search for their natural parents is another favorite Movie of the Week subject, which at least gives us a few insights into the people (women) who gave up their babies.

Lately, we've been moving into other movie narratives with harsher – more secret, more violent, more tragic – scenarios: stories of wife-battering, child and elder abuse, rape and incest, and even murder. They're more than movies of the week; these are real life events.

PART THREE

WHEN FAMILIES GO BAD

9

Violence

WIVES/MATES

Violence has been a part of family life for as long as there have been families. The family, in fact, has entrenched violence and reinforced it. Talk about self-fulfilling prophecies! Family as an institution has perpetuated violence. Women, particularly, have been trained (brainwashed?) to believe that the family is sacrosanct. Our institutions and social service agencies believe it, too, and in their efforts to preserve the sanctity and the privacy of the home, also help to perpetuate the violence within it. For sanctity read "control." For privacy read "isolation." Surely the sanctity and the privacy that keep women and children imprisoned and tortured in their homes are not worth preserving.

No one lives in a vacuum, although some families come close. Private life, assaulted as it is by outside influences, remains private. Families, of course, are very private. Ultimately, no one knows what goes on behind closed doors. Until very recently, no one wanted, or presumed to. Lately, it has been in the interests of the well-being of families that the community take an interest in what is going on.

It is to the everlasting and recorded shame of the House of Commons in Canada that as recently as 1982, when MP Margaret Mitchell (Vancouver-East) made a motion to address the problem of wife battering, she was met with laughter and ridicule. *The men laughed.* Wife abuse is not a joke.

It is to the everlasting credit of Canada that it was the first country in the world to make it a crime for a husband to rape his wife. Canada was also the first country in the world (in 1983) to pass a nationwide policy instructing police to lay charges against batterers. Unfortunately, we have lagged since then, because they can't make the charges stick without the testimony of the victim, who too often recants out of fear or dependency, and also for the simple, incontrovertible fact of love. Sad but true that love closes one's eyes more tightly than punches.

When the Canadian Advisory Council on the Status of Women published its first report on wife beating by Linda McLeod in 1980, *Wife Battering in Canada: The Vicious Circle* met with disbelief. The shocking estimate then that one in ten wives was abused was actually too low, and just a guess. It was drawn in 1978 from the very few transition houses and hostels (the ones that accepted battered women) across Canada, 73 at that time; from divorce applications that cited physical cruelty in their grounds; and from police calls for help from battered women. One study estimated that there were ten unreported cases for every call actually made. (U.S. studies based on household surveys about the same time suggested that even the one-in-ten estimate was probably conservative.) The point was that domestic violence was more common than hitherto believed.

In June, 1987, the Advisory Council published a new report. *Battered but Not Beaten*, also by Linda McLeod, met with anger this time, not disbelief. After all the fuss and the effort to get rid of the problem, people (politicians? the media? men?) challenged the new and even more depressing statement that one million (one in eight) Canadian women were battered. Everyone preferred that the victims remained invisible, as they had done over the centuries.

According to the 1993 Violence Against Women Survey, 29 percent of Canadian women (or 2.7 million) who had ever been married or lived common law had been physically or sexually assaulted by their partner at some point during the relationship – frequently when it was supposed to be over. Exes – husbands and commonlaws – weren't through with them yet. Even teenage girls were getting beaten or raped by their boyfriends. All are victims of assault.

Women account for one-third of all homicide victims in Canada (1991 statistics), but they make up almost two-thirds of all homicide victims killed in a domestic relationship. These are women murdered by their spouses or ex-lovers, that is, by someone they know intimately. (The woman who kills her husband is usually discovered to be an assaulted wife, responding after years of abuse with a final, desperate act.)

I have not even mentioned emotional abuse with or without physical violence. I'm dealing with spousal assault here. An assault is defined as an incident where the violent partner could be charged under Canada's Criminal Code. In 1993, few women (25 percent) in abusive relationships reported the violence to police. And of those on record, few of them (24 percent) used support agencies, and those who did preferred an individual counselor to a shelter. Women were more likely to turn to social agencies only when they had been injured or when their children witnessed the assault. Most of them turned first for help to family, friends and neighbors.

Many women never tell anyone. What good would it do? Here is the kind of answer some of them receive.

"My pastor's wife told me that I should keep forgiving him."

"My mother told me that when I left home, I wouldn't be coming back for help every time we had a fight."

"She told me to go ahead and call the police, and when the school district found out that I had a woman lover, I would not have to worry about teaching school [here] again" (proving that not all the abusive relationships are heterosexual).

Further investigation shows that for every battered woman there's probably one or more seriously disturbed children who have had to witness the bashing. Sometimes they are forced to share in it, not only to be on the receiving end themselves, which happens, but also to participate in their mother's "punishment."

Wife battering hasn't lessened in the years since the 1993 survey was taken. However, male-dominated federal and provincial governments, in the interests of lowering their deficits, are cutting services and shelters and funds for controlling violence against women. From a standing start in 1970, the number of shelters for abused women increased to almost 350 by 1993, but the number is decreasing now as they are being shut down.

The idea is – if it *is* an idea – that families will take care of their own. Wife battering is, after all, a family matter, isn't it? Not to be mentioned in polite society. Indeed, it isn't – in polite society. It is seen as a problem belonging to the lower-class, blue-collar or unemployed sector, the crack-cocaine or alcohol addicts who lurch in and out of jobs and solve problems with their fists or a broken beer bottle. While 40 percent of batterers today are unemployed, well above the present high rate of unemployment, that means *60 percent of them are not.* One report (from a survey in Winnipeg) reveals that the three most common occupations of batterers are truck driver, police officer and doctor. Maybe it's the cold weather. It really is almost impossible to generalize, except for this: anyone who doesn't help to eliminate the violence becomes an accomplice to the crimes.

I have a dear friend who has been in and out of mental hospitals for many years of her adult life. As a child, she regularly witnessed her mother's beatings, and her siblings, and she herself suffered cruelly at the brutal hands of her father. One of her sisters was a certain victim of incest. Lyn (not her real name) suspects her father did strange things to her at bath time but she has been blessed with a selective amnesia. When her father died she was horribly shaken by his death. She wanted to go and deliver – no, shout – a funeral oration that would tell the world what he was really like, what he had done to his family. She didn't. She stayed away.

I have another friend I'll call Sandra, one of the wealthy ones who never become part of the statistical profile (poverty is not the only cause of violence, though it is a catalyst). Her husband started beating her when she was pregnant with their first child. Another statistic: 80 percent of beaten women are beaten during pregnancy. In fact, pregnancy has been cited as one of the major incitements to violence. Sandra was too ashamed to admit her *failure* to anyone. Note: women usually blame themselves, not their husband. In Sandra's case, she had the means to leave, but social pressure kept her home, and quiet. She drank instead, a lot. She hid from the world and drowned her troubles in a bottle of sherry. After her husband died, she dried out.

Middle-class women are not better off, in fact, they have more to lose, both financially and socially. Their friends and families would prefer them not to air their dirty linen in public; they themselves can't stand the thought of applying for social assistance or support. "Only tacky, lower-class people go to shelters or seek welfare." So they remain quiet, and their husbands are usually careful to make sure the bruises won't show when they get dressed to go out.

Men beat their women for the simplest of reasons: they can. They always have; why should they quit? Let it be acknowledged that there are cases of husband battering by belligerent wives. However, their assaults do not cause the kinds of life-threatening injuries suffered by women at the hands of their men. In the patriarchal family, the head of the household assumes what amounts to his divine right. Until very recently his behavior has been morally justified and upheld by ancient tradition. In "A Social History of Battered Women," cited in *Wife Battering in Canada*, Mary Metzger reports that "the first known written law, thought to date from about 2500 B.C., proclaimed that the name of any woman who verbally abused her husband was to be engraved on a brick which was then to be used to bash out her teeth."

The first marriage laws, enacted by Romulus around 753 B.C., described married women's position: "as having no other refuge, to conform themselves entirely to the temper of their husbands, and the husbands to rule their wives as necessary and inseparable possessions."

As late as 1663 in England, a man was legally entitled to beat his wife. The expression "rule of thumb" comes from the tradition of wife beating. In the 19th century, British law stated that a husband could "chastise" his wife with "any reasonable instrument... a rod not thicker than his thumb" (from *No Safe Place*, Guberman and Wolfe, eds.).

And as late as Christmas, 1987, a Salvation Army gift shop in Ontario was selling handcrafted wooden paddles for wife beating. At least by then consciousness had been raised to the point that, after an item on the evening news brought the paddles to public attention, they were removed from the market, though the Sally Ann spokes*man* was regretful because he felt such a ban would discourage the "creativity" of the crafts*men*.

In spite of overwhelming statistics supporting my argument, I am all too aware of the danger of generalizations. Of course, there are caring, gentle men and we honor and love them. Of course, there are cruel and violent women. I know that there are often social reasons for violence in both sexes: unemployment, poverty, illness, stress, alcoholism, crack-cocaine. Surely these are only excuses, not valid causes.

Men's sole, rightful cause is still *be-cause*. They can do it and they keep on doing it and they keep on getting away with doing it. What is it about our society that seems to reward power and brute force? Religion, laws, centuries of entrenched behavior have given men what they think is their right to punch out their women. Never mind who gave them that right. We have to take it away. A man has no right to call his home his castle if it is also his wife's torture chamber.

For all classes, if the woman is going to change her life, it seems she is the one who must forfeit house, home, family, means, support and position (if any) in society in order to end the battering process. If she decides to exit, that's what it is: ignominious defeat. Escape means banishment while the victor retains the field, that is, the house and the income. I did meet one woman, past middle age (and therefore with little hope of adequate employment income) who told me she finally managed to send her abusive husband from their large, comfortable house, but she had been left with no money to heat it, let alone to eat. Her husband was a skilled accountant and he hid his money in the Cayman Islands. Their family lawyer sent her a bill for $50,000 for trying to get some redress for her – but he could't find the money either. Did he try very hard?

The problem is endemic because violence is a cultural style of our society. We admire – or some people do – power, and by corollary, coercion, force, brute strength. We condone, nay, believe in, physical strength and power as the most effective means of controlling behavior – at least, some people (men) do.

In March, 1996, the *Toronto Star* newspaper published a seven-part in-depth study of spousal abuse by a team of three reporters after eight months of full-time investigative work.*

Taking a sample week in the summer of 1995, and following up on 133 cases of domestic violence (230 charges), they reported the results when 75 percent of the cases had gone to trial (after eight months!). Of these, 40 percent of the accused had been acquitted, mostly because their victims refused to testify or recanted their statements. Of the 60 percent who were convicted, 90 percent of the convictions were obtained through guilty pleas entered after the crown attorney agreed to drop the worst charges. Of the 60 percent found guilty, 23 were jailed, with an average sentence of 30 days (maximum penalties can range up to 14 years) and 37 got off with probation, no jail sentence, and frequently no criminal record after probation. Within a year, 1 in 4 of those charged with domestic assault were charged again; the majority of them attacked the same women.

An anger management program exists in Ontario; 43 percent of the convicted men were ordered to attend, but there's a waiting list of over 8 months. At any given time, an average of 5000 men in Toronto are on probation for domestic assault. There are 120 slots a year in the anger program designed to help men curb a lifetime habit of solving problems with their fists. Counselors question whether these men have such a problem with their so-called uncontrollable anger – they don't get into fights with their bosses or co-workers. Their crimes against their wives and girlfriends are demonstrations of power – *because they can.*

If men over the centuries have had the right and the power and the means to beat their women, they have also enjoyed a continuously ac-

---

* I am indebted to Jane Armstrong, Rita Daly, and Caroline Mallan for their thorough, detailed, and moving report, and for the damning follow-up indicating the horrifying repetition of crimes which went unpunished.

cessible, vulnerable target. Women have had no place to go, nowhere to escape from their domestic despots. Over the centuries they have been held firmly in place by their economic dependence and also by society's sanctions that subliminally permit a husband to "control" his wife. Cases that came to public attention, even desperate calls to the police or other authorities over the last century, were by and large hushed up, settled privately, ignored. Until that 1983 law requiring the police to lay charges (and even since), police have traditionally not liked to interfere in a "domestic dispute," claiming the sanctity of the home and a man's right to privacy as their reasons not to meddle.

Frequently still, wives prefer not to prosecute or else withdraw their statements. One reason is that they still love their man; another is they have no place to go and no support, especially if they have children. There's a worse reason. Battering husbands work like the Mafia: if a victim complains of her treatment, she gets worse. On the other hand, if a wife should "succeed" and the guy is thrown into jail, what has she gained? If the breadwinner goes to jail, what happens to the family dependent on him? The double income at least has given some leverage to a working wife who wants to leave. It may be possible, that is, if she has a job, and if her children haven't been threatened. (Almost one-third of assaults on mothers of children are witnessed by the children.)

In the case of a severed relationship, the vengeful accused man may begin systematically stalking and harassing the woman. Although an anti-stalking law was passed in June, 1993, whereby the man is not supposed to be within 500 feet of the woman and to lay off, a determined abuser will stop at nothing, including murder. In many cases, the man is back with the threats within hours of the court case, whether or not he has had a peace bond hung over him. Some experts believe a $300 or $500 fine, payable upon breaking the promise, or bond, to keep the peace with the victim, is worthless, and the victims live in constant fear. "I have this feeling," one woman is reported as saying, "I'm sure that I'm going to be one of the women that you read about in the newspaper after she's murdered."

In most of North America, a man does not even go to jail for beating his wife, and he does it again. One city has begun to make real strides in the prevention of the crime and the protection of the woman. San Diego won't take no for an answer from a wife who recants. The police are not only empowered to lay charges, as they are in Canada, but they are also permitted to use the woman's initial statement on the night (usually night) of the assault; their own obligatory detailed reports; testimony from other witnesses; photographs they are required to take of her injuries at the time; and the recording of the 911 distress call, if there was one. This evidence holds up in court and enables conviction.

The conviction rate in San Diego, as of 1995, is a hefty 95 percent, as compared to Toronto's 60 percent. The American city's convicted batterers must attend a 34-week program to help control their anger, for which they must pay $10 a session. The number of repeat offenders is lower than Toronto's and the domestic murder rate has dropped by half. It's a beginning worth copying.

In May of 1996 Metro Toronto police announced plans to use more thorough evidence-gathering procedures in domestic disputes, modeling their methods after San Diego's crime reports. As of November of that year, nothing had changed. (The word was that funds had not come through.)

In July of 1996, Metro Toronto's downtown crown prosecutors called for a special court to deal exclusively with spousal abuse, to begin operating in the fall. By November, it was scheduled to begin hearing cases in January, 1997. I hope it has.

CODA

Judge Ronald J. Meyers is a family court judge presiding at the Family Violence Court in Winnipeg. He was the first and used to be the only judge who sat in this court on a full-time basis and considered it an opportunity to do what no other judge in Canada had ever done – play a major role in stopping the abuse of women. Apart from the shortcomings in the system, he soon realized that its main players (the Crown and judges) would have to develop an awareness and understanding of the plight of the victims. There are now more than a dozen judges who, after an initial reluctance, have been "sensitized" and take their turn. Critics question Meyer's impartiality, accusing him of becoming an advocate. He accepts that. "Making changes in the status quo," he says, "is not easy."

Where did this privileged and powerful man gain his own sensitivity? He says that he grew up in a home where he witnessed the constant abuse of his mother by his father. It convinced him that outside intervention is necessary and that the criminal justice system has to be involved.

We can't allow the family to be the last holdout in the system.

GRANNY BASHING

It's the weak who get ripped off.
– Alex Comfort

Both women and men are guilty of another kind of abuse going on in the home, that of "granny bashing." Again, however, according to statistics, more men than women beat up their parents – usually one parent, old, dependent, a drag.

This is where we really separate Norman Rockwell from reality. Old people in the American artist's illustrations are depicted as happy, healthy, solving a problem for a grandchild, or sitting in the midst of a large, loving family – although come to think of it, that grandparent is usually male. The grandmas are in the kitchen, making pie.

If the grandpas are still around, their old ladies are not doing too badly. Old men have a higher income than old women and tend to share it with women who look after them. But women far outnumber men among the older population; 74 percent of them are single (bereaved, divorced, never married) and 40 percent (down from 65 percent) of them live below the Low Income Cut-Off, as Stats Can euphemistically calls the poverty line. Even so, senior single women are more likely to live alone than their younger counterparts (38 percent of those over 65, compared with 12 percent of women 45–64), and twice as likely to be alone as men their age (the men are either still married or dead). However, a significant number of senior women live with some part of their family; in 1991, 11 percent of women over 65 lived with other relatives (compared with 4 percent of senior men), and this is what puts them at risk.

The physical abuse of elders is not news, but it didn't get much attention before the 1980s, although it is defined by sociologists as a major type of "intimate violence." We're paying more attention now for several reasons. One, there are more "elders" around and their numbers are increasing as more people are living into old age. Two, they didn't prepare for it – or couldn't – with adequate retirement plans, so their middle-aged children have to look after them, and that puts additional pressure on the family. Three, seniors vote. Actually they vote in elections more than other age groups, so somebody (read "government") has to pay attention to them. Four, the experts are getting more and more interested in the criminal victimization of the elderly.

This victimization concludes with violence but doesn't begin there. Apart from emotional, psychological abuse, which I haven't touched on and which is inflicted on wives, lovers and children as well, elders are also victims of financial abuse. Outsiders keep thinking up new ways to con seniors out of their dollars with scare tactics or get-rich-quick schemes; family members simply take their money (those who have money), get them to change their wills, or charge outrageously for minimal services rendered.

No one, not even the experts, can accurately determine the extent of the physical abuse of elderly family members. Older people don't just fall between the cracks of the social system; there *is* no system, at least, none that they are connected to. They're not out in the community where their bruises may be *seen*, in fact, They're probably confined to the house (or sometimes locked in a room) with no one to observe what's going on. Also, they are reluctant to report violence, or too frail or vague or fearful of reprisals or of alternative living arrangements. Then, too, even if they live apart from their "loved ones" that doesn't exempt them from family abuse. It does, however, make them more vulnerable to attack by young strangers. The newspapers regularly report muggings and even murder of lonely old people – usually women by street kids looking for easy drug money.

Leah Cohen published a book in 1984 that is still in print in paperback. *Small Expectations: Society's Betrayal of Older Women* was a devastating indictment and it's more valid than ever. It is still a shameful secret, seldom acknowledged even by the victims, who blame themselves. We have begun to be aware of their poverty; what hasn't sunk in is their use as punching bags. As indicated, violence against older women has not been well documented. Cohen was in the vanguard of data gatherers. She found four areas of violence against older women: familial abuse, institutional and social-services abuse, crime, and wife battering. I am concerned here with what goes on in the family.

As we have seen, wife battering is very democratic, paying no heed to income or status. Why should it stop at age?

> You would think I would be used to it by now – it's gone
> on for more than 50 years.

– A 72-year-old woman

It still goes on. How can anyone get used to it, even after 50 years? It becomes an even more shameful secret with advancing years, and harder to escape. The average age of a battered wife who seeks shelter is late 20s, early 30s. Shelters are not designed for older women. The stairs are steep, the doors are heavy, the noise levels of the children (of the younger women) are too loud. Where can an older woman go? With few relatives and friends (moved away, died off) and even fewer resources, and no possible means of supporting herself if she does escape, where can she turn?

The 72-year-old quoted above spoke to her father once, when she was younger and tried to leave her alcoholic, abusive husband. He told her a wife belongs to her husband and if a husband beats a wife, it was because "she deserves it." Once also, years later, she spoke to a lawyer; he told her she had better stay where she was. Her doctor noted that her health wasn't too good. She said she tried to tell him about her husband but he didn't want to hear. Even when she needed surgery to stop internal bleeding from a bad beating, "the doctors in the hospital never asked me any questions."

That, at least, has changed. Doctors and hospital officials are starting to ask questions. In the case of a child's injury, it's mandatory, although what happens after that is not always effective follow-up.

Cohen reports another women who, at age 65, finally ran away.

(One is reminded of Constance Beresford-Howe's novel, *Book of Eve*, which recounts the adventures of a woman who runs away from her marriage on the day she receives her first Old Age Security check. The new Senior Benefit Reform will no longer make it possible for the wife of an affluent husband to leave him because the assessment of need will be based on the couple's combined incomes; there's now such a thing as what I call Upper Income Cut-Off.)

Cohen's runaway had talked to her minister, but he told her that a husband and wife belong together. She had talked to the police; they thought she was exaggerating. After they left, her husband knocked out some of her teeth. In a boarding house when Cohen talked to her, she was glad that she was finally free.

"Being free," she said, "is more important than my share of the house and our savings."

What happens to old women in a family context? Women are even more reluctant to talk about that. "No one ever thinks a child of hers will behave so badly," says one old woman. When she was younger and healthy her son was kind to her but after her husband died she became a burden to him. He beat her, locked her in her room with one meal a day until her bruises healed, beat her again until she was so weak and demoralized that her doctor decided she should move into a nursing home – her son's intention. The television show *Sixty Minutes* showed a film taken by a hidden camera in which nursing home attendants were slam-dunking their patients out of the wheel chairs into their beds! That's another story.

Sons take over, it seems, where their fathers leave off. But daughters are not above cruelty to their aging mothers, only they do it more frequently with verbal abuse and psychological blows.

This didn't happen in the "good old days," we say. In times gone by, old people were the Wise Ones, revered in the community, the holders of ancient wisdom. Uh huh. Too many novels and movies. In the Middle Ages, the old women may indeed have been the repositories of useful knowledge: herbs and medications, abortifacients, natural pain relievers. Maybe. It's hearsay now because most of them were killed – burned or drowned as witches. Who can say what they knew? They weren't revered long enough to pass on the lore.

Even in this century old people didn't used to be very old, not many of them. The average life expectancy of a woman at the turn of the century was only 48 years because women died so regularly in childbirth. Now with antisepsis and improved nutrition, women are living longer than their men folk and outliving their support system. So who's going to take care of them?

Granny bashing is not the answer.

10

Spare the Rod and Spoil the Child

*He is teaching me he says. This is what it means to be a
woman. Drop your panties. Lean over the bench. Take
your beating. Don't whimper and snivel. Don't cry. If you
cry he beats harder and longer. It pleases him to hit you.
He looks forward to it. Don't turn around. He doesn't
want you to see how much it pleases him.*

– Elly Danica

ABUSE

If men used to have inviolate rights over their wives, they had even more over
their children – the unquestioned, absolute power of life and death. Until the
invention of childhood (see Philippe Ariès) children were, to put it mildly,
expendable. Scholars trace infanticide back to the biblical period, and earlier.

Parent-to-child violence is not new, but the attention being paid to it
is. As I have been writing this book, a major investigation has been called
for into the deaths by neglect and abuse of young children. A couple in
Ontario have both received stiff sentences for the beating death of a six-
month-old baby girl whose body showed evidence of earlier trauma.
Another couple in New Brunswick were also recently convicted in the
death by starvation of their four-year-old boy.

Questions arise: Where was the Children's Aid Society? (Its decisions
and effectiveness are being reviewed.) But where, also, was the commu-

nity? Why didn't neighbors respond to the screams of an infant being beaten to death? Why didn't neighbors step in when they saw a child starving? Protection laws in every province, except in the Yukon where it is not mandatory, now require people to report cases of suspected child abuse or neglect to the authorities – family services, police, etc.

The Kids Help Phone Line is a national toll-free, confidential bilingual hot line operating 24 hours a day, seven days a week, for children and adolescents who need help (see Appendix, p. 226). I have already mentioned the Block Parents program, but that's for danger on the streets; we're dealing now with the terror within the home.

I've already confessed to being, like Pearl Buck, a "kiss-and-slap" mother. Actually, I didn't slap, but I yelled a lot and I hit things. Once, when I was emphasizing my point by pounding a bed with a plastic baseball bat, I caught then two-year-old John on a back swing as he came into the room behind me. It took the wind out of him, and of me. Oh my! I can remember the event vividly and so can my children, to this day. But what was the misdemeanor that I was being so adamant about? I can't remember. Was I abusive? Yes.

An American couple was charged during the summer of 1996 in Toronto for physical violence to their child over and above what onlookers deemed to be fair punishment. They had thrown their little girl over the hood of the car and spanked her bare backside hard and too many times. They actually had to appear in court; it wrecked their vacation. They said they weren't coming back to Canada. I wonder if they plan on beating their child again.

Most North Americans don't think of physical punishment of a child as abuse unless it injures a child's health – mentally or physically. They think of "minor" forms of punishment as "necessary, normal, and good." So we have to define abuse: that which causes pain and suffering. There is no accurate measure of it, nor of the extent of it in Canada. We do know, from the most extreme cases which come to light in the media, too late to do the small victim any good, that parent-to-child violence is a serious problem. I won't go into the terrifying and ominous statistics, or the nature of the damage inflicted. This is a family book.

What happens in the family? Or what happened? One of the most consistent discoveries by the researchers is that violence is learned. Children who grow up in violent homes learn to abuse their children when they become parents. The theory is that "violence begets violence."

A little girl who's been beaten promises herself that when she grows up she won't touch her kids. But when she's got three young kids, a husband who's away a lot, not enough money or time, and she's overworked, tired, harassed, with no other examples to go by, she gets physical and lays it on the kids, doing to them what she learned how to do at an early age. People rerun the tapes of what they learn in their childhood. R. D. Laing was right.

People also learn to justify what they do. "This is for your own good," they say. "This hurts me more than it does you," they say. "I'm only doing this because I love you," they say. "You asked for it," they say. "It's just I can't bear to see you act like that," they say. And these are often the same words they use when they hit their spouses.

But we can't blame the family of origin entirely. If we did that, we'd go right back to Adam and Eve. Where did Cain learn to be so violent? Lots of people who come from non-violent homes go on to abuse their wives and children, and lots of people who had direct, hands-on experience, as it were, don't touch their families. A family may be a training ground for abuse, but it's not the only one these days. Everyone is so fond of bashing television that it's almost a cliché, but there's enough violence on it to desensitize a nun. In a piece in *The New Yorker*, American film critic David Denby analyzes the effects on his own sons and wonders about his role. He writes, "If parents are not to feel defeated by the media and pop culture, they must get over their reluctance to make choices that are based on clear assertions of moral values."

I remember a few years ago when *Miami Vice* was all the rage on American television, cited for the Armani clothes the detectives wore and for the fine jazz soundtrack, my son John, by then a father, turned it on one night to see what all the fuss was about – and turned it off. He said any so-called entertainment that showed a woman cowering under a bed trying to protect her young son from a couple of vicious thugs with guns was not the kind of thing he wanted to watch. He made a choice without a V-chip.

So are we going to blame the media, peer groups, society at large for the violence in families? It's a huge problem. It begins at home, and not only with the parents. Kids also learn violence from their siblings.

SIBLING VIOLENCE

> *Contempt for younger siblings often hides envy of them...*
> *Contempt also may serve as a defense against other*
> *feelings.*
> – Alice Miller

I have already mentioned the envy that siblings harbor for each other and the secret feeling that the other(s) enjoyed preference over oneself. Does this account for the physical violence siblings inflict on each other?

I used to cringe at the stories my husband told me of his sufferings at the hands of his brother who was eight years older. That's when I learned about knuckle sandwiches and Indian burns and fart suffocation. But I can remember, too, a near concussion when my brother threw a stool at my head, and a circle of blood in my face when he pressed the funnel of his model train into it. (Was I that insufferable as to provoke such actions?

Don't blame the victim!) Is this all a normal part of growing up?

M. A. Straus and R. J. Gelles (sociologists specializing in family research) state that children are the most violent members of all American families. And not only American, if the violence described in Roddy Doyle's prize-winning book, *Paddy Clarke, Ha Ha Ha* is to be believed. Some of the horrible things the older brother, the protagonist of the story, did to his little brother left permanent damage. I know someone whose little brother died during a vicious pillow fight, but that was an accident, wasn't it? We all know tales of play gone wrong.

If it's so common, why hasn't anyone done anything about it, or even talked about it? Gelles and Cornell, in a book about *Intimate Violence in Families*, cite several reasons. One is that siblings hitting each other happens so often that no one thinks they're violent; it's just part of growing up. Parents don't discourage the fighting as such, just the noise. They don't take sides, unless the smallest one is getting hurt – or yells too loudly. A second reason is that rivalry within the family is considered healthy, or at least normal, and good training for the cutthroat competition in the real world. (This isn't real?) Three is that everyone expects kids to fight, so no one worries about it. I'd add a fourth, that parents don't usually "see" or comprehend the depth and extent of sibling violence.

The myth is that siblings usually grow up to be good friends but I don't buy that, either. It has been my observation that if they were at each other's throats when they were kids they still resent each other as adults; they're just a little more polite, is all. None of this is trivial.

I've cited American researchers (as quoted in *Families* by Maureen Baker). The only Canadian report on this kind of family violence was undertaken in 1994 by D. Ellis and W.S. DeKeseredy for Health Canada (Family Violence Prevention). In an admittedly limited survey, the two sociologists found that 47.8 percent of a small group of university undergraduates interviewed and 100 percent of a smaller group of (learning-disabled) children said they had been physically victimized by their siblings. The researchers admitted that they were aware that collecting information from learning disabled children doesn't provide any valid basis for generalizing to all children. However, the sample children were chosen to determine the *patterning* of hurtful sibling interactions; to get that Ellis and DeKeseredy deliberately selected a group in which this kind of interaction occurred quite frequently. They asked for simple descriptions of fights, problems with brothers or sisters, and the kind of hurt the children suffered – feelings or bruises.

Since it is such an underdeveloped area of research, little or no theory has evolved about sibling violence. It's possible that children who have witnessed marital violence or who have been physically assaulted by their parents learn the behavior. My husband's mother was a gentle widow; where did his brother learn it? It has also been observed that lots of kids who have seen wife/mother beating and experienced it themselves *don't* resort to violence with their brothers and sisters. Other factors to be considered: learning difficulties; physical handicaps; size and strength; little interaction with parents; marital separation; inconsistent discipline; father's criminal record; poverty.

Hold that thought.

SEXUAL ABUSE

Incest: the crime of sexual intercourse between persons so closely related that their marriage is prohibited by law.
– Gage Canadian Dictionary

Don't touch children where they don't want to be touched.
– Children's Rules for Parents

Canadian statistics, as of 1995, indicate that one in two females and one in three males have been victims of an unwanted sexual act at some time during their lives, many of them when they were infants, toddlers, or preschoolers, most before they were 13, the rest by age 18. Put it this way: it's as common as wearing glasses; 51 percent of kids over the age of three need prescription lenses. As to the offenders, 85 percent of them are someone the child knows and is supposed to be able to trust.

Intercourse isn't the whole story; other traumatic acts can and do take place. The victim, as has been noted, may be male. There are frequently three persons involved, the third being the non-participating parent who may turn a blind eye and a deaf ear or blame the child rather than the other parent – who is frequently a stepfather or a surrogate, i.e. common-law spouse.

Among the common physical problems caused by adult-child sex are "cases of rectal fissures, lesions, poor sphincter control, lacerated vaginas, foreign bodies in the anus and vagina, perforated anal and vaginal walls, death by asphyxiation, chronic choking from gonorrheal tonsillitis," to name a few. (This list is taken from "Child Sexual Assault" by Alanna Mitchell, in *No Safe Place*.) Not surprisingly, there are emotional side effects as well: repressed rage, feelings of powerlessness and fear, lack of trust, low self-esteem – being "damaged goods" – guilt feelings, depression, alienation.

It's estimated that about half of all prostitutes were sexually abused as children. It has also been established that many battered women are survivors of childhood sexual abuse. Abused as children and witnesses of their mothers' beatings at the hands of their fathers, they received an early message: to accept, and even support the violence men do to women and children. The flaw in this is that of seeing the victim as cause, the idea that victims seek out a repetition of their childhood patterns. Have they really been "trained" or brainwashed into it? I hope not.

I'm beginning to think I'm an exception to the staggering statistics; I'm the other one out of two who was *not* sexually abused as a child. In my sheltered rearing, I never even heard of incest until I read Norse mythology and Inca history in my late teens. My first close-up knowledge came in a story from my father, who was a family physician. He didn't know about it, either, at least not in one particular case. It came to light long after the initial events.

A woman I'll call Joyce had been his patient her entire life; he had delivered her into the world and then her children as well. When her oldest daughter was 12, Joyce finally asked my father for help with a lifelong problem. Turned out her father had used her sexually when she was a girl, and now, an old man, living with his daughter's family, he was using his granddaughter. Joyce might have tolerated this and let her daughter suffer as she had, but the old man was extending his attentions to her daughter's girl friend and Joyce was terrified that there would be repercussions (like the police) once the problem went out of the family.

My father was astounded; he thought he knew his patient so well. Why hadn't Joyce ever told him? It was private, she said, family business. Besides, would he have believed her? (There has always been a lot of denial flying around about incest, both within and without the family circle.) She wouldn't have told him then but for the risk of it going public. My father wanted to know how it had affected her. She got out early, she said, that's why she left home and married so young, to get away from her father. It was too bad, she said, that her mother had died and not her father, but someone had to take him in. Blood is thicker than water.

My father used to say, "I don't know where I was when they took this up at medical school. I must have missed that day." We all did. No one talked about it then. Decades-old cases of abuse in schools and institutions are only now coming to light as men and women, psychically scarred for life, are telling their stories. How much harder to accuse one's own family! It's not a suddenly fashionable trauma that has only begun to occur. It happened, but we just didn't talk about it. Incest is one of the biggest taboos of our society. That's not to say the taboo isn't broken, and not only the taboo – lives are broken too.

Several years ago I went to a feminist weekend and took part in an astonishing seminar one evening. Of nine women gathered in a small group to discuss pornography, three of them had been sexually abused in their early or late childhood. That's 33 percent, one in three of a random sample. Close.

One, the lucky one, was raped by a stranger when she was 13. Though she was an only child and her parents older than average, shocked, and embarrassed by the event, the situation was handled well. The girl was encouraged to tell her story to the police, who listened, and she was given counseling. She went into a caring profession herself, eventually married a gentle man, and found her own motherhood to be a healing process. She wrote a woman's prayer for us that weekend that I still have.

Another, younger woman was molested over some period of time when she was 15, by a member of her family she would not identify. One got the impression that she had been emotionally blackmailed into continuing acquiescence. When she finally broke away by leaving home, she said she became "a man-hater and a cock-teaser." She had to control the sex act with any man who came near her, and often sought out strangers to prove to herself that she had power over them. She married in her late 20s and discovered to her sorrow that her uterus had been damaged and she was unable to bear children. She and her husband adopted a baby girl, who was a great comfort and joy. But the marriage didn't survive and the woman was on a knife-edge when I met her, her past trauma still unresolved.

She said she had intended to kill her four-year-old daughter and herself and had even bought a pretty dress for her daughter to wear for the occasion. Something happened that weekend, however, that made her change her mind. She said that a door had opened and she could see some light. Talking helps. Professional therapy is even better.

The third woman, 20 years old and youngest of the three, pretty but very fat, had only recently confirmed her suspicions about the abuse of her body. It had been buried in her memory, like a time bomb ticking away, getting ready to destroy her. Her father had raped her in her crib when she was not more than 18 months old. All the bad dreams in her childhood, all her self-hatred, her inability to be alone in the same room with her father, her anger, her eating problems, her destructive relationships with men, remained unexplained until, just a year before I met her, she had undergone gestalt hypnosis and relived what had been done to her. She dredged up from her subconscious memory what she described as "Hiroshima – a blood bath." She confronted her father with her discovery and he admitted what he had done. She turned to women for her comfort.

Mary Lea Johnson, an heir to the Johnson and Johnson pharmaceutical fortune, described, in an issue of *Ms.* magazine, her incestuous abuse by her father from the time she was nine until she was 15. She didn't tell the story for almost 50 years, until she finally realized that it wasn't her fault.

"Sexual abuse can happen in any family," says Johnson, "rich or poor, black or white, city or country."

Canada too.

Why don't more women complain, blow the whistle on their husbands? First of all, they, like society, don't want to believe that what is happening is really happening. If their daughters – or sons – try to tell them, they hush them or blame them. Often they feel they have no choice. They are dependent on their husbands, they have no support system, there are other children who need them. They are helpless, they think, unable to protect the child. Often they were victims of some kind of childhood sexual assault themselves. It is estimated that between 25 and 35 percent of people who were abused as children mistreat their own children.

It is not, however, obligatory for history to repeat itself. It has to stop some time. If the mothers have been abused themselves, and been unable to face up to their own past trauma, how can they deal with their children's? It must *not* be self-perpetuating. What happens to these children?

I can't help thinking about Lolita, the child victim in Nabokov's book of the same name. She had absolutely no curiosity about, no interest whatsoever in sex. Her adolescent peers had reached the experimental stage, not her. If there is no spark, no sign of normal wonder, about sex, then the lack of interest should be questioned. Other signs to watch for:

➤ poor sleeping habits
➤ migraine headaches
➤ depression
➤ bad eating habits
➤ loss of friends
➤ listlessness
➤ physical symptoms.

Professionals have to realize that they must do something about the sexual abuse of children – at least persuade the child to talk about it. Get her away her from her offender if at all possible. Better yet, get the offender away from her – him. Little boys are victims, too.

Cruelty to children was made punishable under English law *60 years after* the criminalization of cruelty to animals.

11

Poverty

Come away; poverty's catching.
– Aphra Behn

It seems to be human nature to assume that bad things happen to other people, not us. We think we're immortal until proved otherwise. We think we are exempt, safe from life's trauma, or if not safe, at least sheltered and fed. Poverty, whether or not we experience it firsthand, is a reality to many Canadians. It's dangerous, it affects all of us – families, society. Poverty is a violation of human rights.

"The poor are always with us," as the prophet said, but he had a few suggestions for solving the problem of poverty, none of which has ever been taken seriously (like, "Sell all you have and give to the poor," like, "Lay not up treasures on this earth," like, "Inasmuch as ye have done it to the least of these, ye have done it to me"). Our male-dominated governments are much more practical.

Quite apart from the lower-income sector of our society, whose problems will engulf us all if we don't do something, the source of the tax moneys, the foundation of family values, the heart beat of the nation (I sound like an easy-rock radio station!) – in short, the middle class – is suffering. It is also shrinking, its numbers reduced by over one percent in the last decade, and its income in real dollars also reduced and shrinking steadily. To put this in digestible terms: for every 12 middle-class families in 1980, there are only 11 now – 275,000 fewer families with less discretionary income than before.*

Double-income families, as might be expected, do better than single-earner families; two-parent families, even with one paycheck, are way ahead of single-parent ones, most of them headed by women. Between 1989 and 1993, two-parent families' incomes dropped by 8 percent while single-parent families' incomes plunged by 23 percent. By 1994 (the last statistics available, according to *Perspectives on Labour and Income*, compiled by Susan Crompton and published by Statistics Canada, August, 1996), the market income of two-parent families was a little higher than it was in 1982 whereas the income of one-parent families was 17 percent lower. No wonder lone-parent families rely on welfare and other government assistance. Even adding the income from these sources, they're worse off now than in 1980.

They're young, too, younger than ever. In 1980, 20 percent of the heads of low-income families were under 24; by 1994 a staggering 44 percent of them were that young. Any bets on how many are female?

People seem to be squeamish about referring to the poverty line as such. It's called Low-Income Cut-Off (LICO). What it means is that low-income earners spend more than 54.7 percent of their income on necessities like food, shelter and clothing. They're called the working poor. The ever-widening gap between income and outgo has been (par-

---

* These figures taken from "The Death of the Middle Class," by Daphne Bramhan and Gordon Hamilton, *Transition*, March, 1993.

tially) alleviated by higher transfer payments (that is, welfare, UI, child tax, goods and services tax credits). But what of the unemployed?

Contrary to public opinion, the numbers of permanent welfare recipients are not huge. The estimate is that 5 percent of families are chronically poor, that is, poverty runs in the family, from one generation to the next. The other names and numbers keep shifting as people move in and out of jobs – or marriage. The chief reasons for becoming poor are the addition of a family member (one child or children too many, a disabled adult, an aging parent), job loss, and family breakdown (divorce, separation, widowhood). Most people try desperately to get back on track, finding new jobs, moonlighting, going after new skills to earn more money.

Poor people keep shifting – I don't mean moving, I mean their names change. Their faces don't, they all look anxious, not to say terrified, bleak, defeated.

According to psychologist Camil Bouchard, a former member of the Board of Directors of the VIF, "three or four of every ten people who are poor this year will remain poor next year. The others will have ceased to be poor, only to be replaced in the ranks by other families." If governments close some of the escape hatches, such as subsidized day care and new job training, they are condemning people to longer-term, even permanent poverty.

Sooner or later we are going to have to come to terms with poverty, what it means, how it affects people. World statistics indicate that the number of people actually dying of starvation is decreasing. Isn't it ironic that those who survive because of better nutrition and cleaner water live to die in wars caused by the struggle for power? Social scientists agree that much of the world's poverty rises from a lack of power, or of power in the wrong hands. It also rises from a perception of the differences between the haves and the have-nots.

I think that in our world poverty is in the eyes of the beholder, but it is far from being imaginary. Although few, if any, people in North America are as poor or deprived as those in the Third World, their poverty is just as, if not more, demoralizing. Lack of opportunity, lower educational achievement, child hunger and mortality, alcohol and drug abuse and violence may not be caused by poverty, but they are terrible symptoms of it. Surely it is important for us to feed the spirit as well as the need.

Boxing Helena is a movie I didn't see and don't want to. The story, as I understand it, is about a man who cuts off a woman's arms and legs so she can't leave him. He keeps her in a box. That is the image I kept thinking of as the Harris government in Ontario cut day-care subsidies for single parents (read "mothers"), cut their welfare payments by 21 percent, and cut their job training opportunities and subsidies to make sure they couldn't eventually be able to earn their way out of the box. In a special issue of *Ms.* magazine published in the 1970s on the feminization of poverty, Barbara Ehrenreich made the arguable claim that by the year 2000 – not so far away now – all of the poor of North America will be women and their children. I keep asking: what happens to men's children?

On welfare or not, with one or two unemployed or low-income parents, one in five children in Canada is growing up in poverty. Abundant research shows a clear link between violence in the home and poverty. Clearer still is the link between poverty and the physical abuse of children and wives, with a little sexual abuse thrown in as an appetizer. Child abuse is more common in poor families.

Never mind their neglect or lack of opportunity for a decent education or their prospects or the very real possibility that they will swell the ranks of the permanently poor in the future, children are hungry today. Their families can't afford to feed them; governments aren't helping. Food banks – not-for-profit, non-governmental organizations – are a grassroots attempt to fill the gaps: the empty bellies of our children.

The first food bank opened in Edmonton, Alberta, in 1981. Within three years there were 75 food banks in B.C., Alberta, Saskatchewan, Ontario and Quebec and the numbers kept growing, through downturns and recessions, until, by the fall of 1991, there were some 290 food banks officially registered with the Canadian Association of Food Banks. Established in 1986, it supplies 1200 grocery programs and 580 meal programs in more than 300 communities across Canada. This is not counting any Salvation Army Family Services or various communities' efforts at serving Thanksgiving and Christmas dinners, or private efforts by religious groups or hostels assisting battered women, street children, the homeless and others. The point is that most of the funding of food banks comes from private and non-government sources.

I spoke to Julia Bass, the new executive director of the Association. She told me that as of fall, 1996, there are 450 food banks in Canada, serving some three million people. It's hard to come up with an exact figure because the numbers are collected by the month and fluctuate seasonally and regionally. Bass says they are planning a national survey.

What we do know is this: that 40 percent of these hungry people are children, even though children comprise only 25 percent of Canada's population. How long can we go on giving them handouts?

Food banks solicit food from private citizens in their communities, through cooperative gathering by supermarkets and individual events (for example, a concert at which everyone attending is asked to bring a donation to a food bank). Newspapers help by distributing grocery bags, usually with a list of suggested, non-perishable foods to fill them with. Special drives at Thanksgiving, Christmas and Easter encourage individuals to purchase food and share their bounty and blessings. However, the bulk of the food comes from food industry surpluses: food that has been discarded because of mislabeling,

approaching expiry dates, overproduction, and so on. Food proces-
sors, wholesalers, manufacturers, food brokers, retailers and farmers
are not the only sources; some banks buy food in order to provide a
better nutritional balance to their consumers.

I describe later in this book my "Old Lady Caper," when I went to
live on Old Age Security. The first weekend, when I couldn't find a safe
room to rent, I threw myself on the mercies of Nellie's, a women's hostel
in Toronto. It was a Saturday night in late October and we ate food, given
to the hostel, leftover from a Person's Day Banquet I had actually attended the previous Thursday before I went on assignment. (Person's
Day honors the day women became persons in the eyes of the law in
Canada, October 22, 1929, thanks to the efforts of Emily Murphy and the
ruling of the Privy Council in England.) I recognized the food I had paid
for in a previous reincarnation and I mentally paraphrased Hamlet's line
to Horatio: "Thrift, thrift! The person-baked meats did coldly furnish
forth the hostel table."

There wasn't any meat left, though – mostly potatoes, overcooked,
dried up, not many vitamins.

Kids need vitamins. Poor kids aren't as healthy as those who are
better off. They have a lower birth weight and more disabilities; they
suffer more chronic illnesses, are subject to more injuries and are
hospitalized more often. They are at greater risk emotionally as well
as physically, with more psychiatric and stress-related problems,
mostly because of the circumstances that cause them to be poor. We
know by now that more of them drop out of school, not even finish-
ing high school let alone proceeding to post-secondary studies. With
inadequate education and job training they are less likely to be the
self-supporting, taxpaying citizens the country needs in the future.
Surely it is apparent that money spent on them now will mean a great
deal more money saved on them later. The earlier we invest in chil-

dren and their families the better off we all will be.

My husband's mother was widowed when he, the youngest of three children, was nine. She raised her children on an insurance pension of $27 a month by being frugal and taking in boarders – paying members of the family. Bill was a great soccer player and loved the game but couldn't afford equipment. He used to wear cylindrical oatmeal boxes as shin-guards and was nicknamed "Ogilvie." His shins were as pitted as a picket fence. When he was invited onto a tournament team he declined without even telling his mother because he knew there was no money for shoes.

Okay, that was in the depression. Here's a letter from a 14-year-old boy (quoted from *Transition* magazine, June, 1995):

> *I love sports, but I don't participate in anything because we have no money for equipment. We can never do anything because of lack of money. I feel as if it will always be this way.*

Despair is not an easy lesson to learn, nor to forget.

Ontario Arts Council has an Artists-in-the-Schools program whereby a writer, playwright, poet, visual artist, mime, whatever, is sent in to a school, prearranged between the teacher, the class and the artist, to work with the students and create something with them. As a playwright I found myself several years ago in an inner-city school with a split grade one-two class representing nine languages, with English most often the second one. These children were from decent, working-class families, mostly double-income, often latchkey or cared for after school by a non-English-speaking grandparent. Life for them was real and earnest and not much fun.

When I started to play with them, I asked them to imagine things with me, to make up stories, to wrap their minds around magic. The most they could imagine was a dish of ice cream or a big new car. One day I asked them to explain the game of Hopscotch and then wondered aloud what would happen if they landed on a space without a marker. If it opened like a trapdoor, I asked, and they dropped through into another space, what might happen?

Dead silence.

But someone – their teacher? – had warned them about me.

"There goes Mrs. Wylie," one of them finally said, "imagining things again."

We made a play, those 27 children and their teacher and I, and they put it on for the rest of the school and their parents. I missed it because I was out of town so I went back later to talk to them and find out how it went and they told me things. I listened to each one of them and they listened to each other and we shared wonderful secrets and some sad events and even a little magic.

Magic is very difficult to achieve in the midst of poverty. It needs aiding and abetting and outside help.

PART FOUR

DIVORCE

12

Divorce

Being divorced is like being hit by a Mack truck. If you live through it, you start looking very carefully to the right and to the left.
– Jean Kerr

Creative divorce. That was the optimistic title of a book on the subject published in the 1970s, but it glossed over the pain between the rupture and the beginning of a creative approach, if indeed such creation is ever possible. The author himself decided only after he had divorced and re-married that maybe one marriage was enough. (I wonder what his second wife thought of that.) From another standpoint, American writer Adela Rogers St. Johns had a wry commentary about the progression: "I think every woman's entitled to a middle husband she can forget."

It's so common, we think now, everyone is doing it. Indeed, it would seem so with ominous statistics informing us that one in three marriages ends in divorce. The flip side is that some 60 percent of Canadians stay married to each other for life. Statistics like these can tell us whatever we want them to tell us, depending on which side we look.

When I was in the early stages of my widowhood I used to be angry at people who divorced. How could they do that, I wondered furiously, when both parties were still alive and could still speak, have a dialogue, work things out? I know better now. I don't grow much wiser as I grow older but I've seen more, including the end of some stories. Anyway, as one divorcée said to me early on: "At least you know where *your* husband is."

Each case involves a death, whether of a relationship or of a person. Each case involves a terrible loss. Loss is a difficult fact of life to come to terms with. Loss is inexorable, irretrievable, unbearable, and yet it must be borne. Much of what I have said to my bereaved compatriots (becoming a widow really is like moving to another country – a strange, empty one at first) applies to divorced people. Stress is a common denominator.

Even the stress people – psychologists Holmes and Rahe, who score life events from one to 100 for the stress they carry with them, beginning with a traffic ticket (three points) up to the death of a spouse (100 points) – even they now question whether divorce with a score of 75 and bereavement with 100 shouldn't be switched. Certainly the finality of death spells the end of a relationship very clearly; the survivor is left to struggle on with life's problems knowing for certain that that was then and this horror is now. The divorced person is still living and keeps on bleeding, sometimes literally, as we have seen in the case of violent exes, but emotionally too as the parties involved keep on hurting each other whether they intend to or not. Most of the time it's willful.

There are valid reasons for divorce. There are some people who should never have married in the first place; for them divorce is a release. There are others who have overstepped the bounds of permissible behavior and whose mates must leave them in order to survive. Some people think divorces are made in heaven; they claim, wryly, that the happiest days of their lives were the day they were married and the day they divorced.

Perhaps this accounts for the large numbers of divorced people who remarry: they want another happy day.

The question is, how bad is too bad? How bad does it have to be before it's time to call it quits? American writer Mary Kay Blakely suggests a number of reasons why women get divorced, ranging from failed expectations, lack of communication, alcoholism, drug addiction, physical abuse, disagreements about money, differing rates of maturity, different interests, and so on. She doesn't even mention adultery, which used to be the only reason the courts and some churches allowed, and which is still one of the major causes of divorce, though less often cited. Since the changes to the Divorce Act in Canada in 1985, separation is the cause cited in 91 percent of divorces.

Several years after writing that report, Blakely herself had divorced and she described, in another article, one of the best settlement ideas I have ever heard of. She and her ex renegotiate their divorce every two years in order to review their children's situations and whatever new financial and emotional pressures have arisen. That makes excellent sense.

Embittered wives often give up too soon, including their share of the husband's pension, to which they are entitled by law, simply in order to make a clean break and get away, not realizing how much money they will need to support the children. Conversely, the repentant half of a marriage wrecked by infidelity usually wants to pay blood money in order to wash away some of the guilt. It doesn't wash – nor does it last. Too soon, anger and bitterness wipe away any sense of fairness or decency.

American novelist Kurt Vonnegut once commented on a behavior pattern we call common courtesy. He noted that we expect it of people and people expect it of themselves: that they treat strangers with common courtesy. In fact, most of the time when we don't we can be charged with assault or mischief or invasion of privacy or something nasty. But people who were once in love and who promised to love and honor each other forever fail in the most basic forms of common courtesy to their exes. Thwarted, betrayed and angry, they cheat, revile and sometimes punch out their one-time one-and-only. It doesn't make sense.

As society has changed its attitudes and rules, marriage breakdown, as it is called, is supposed to be reason enough to divorce. Some people quit because they're bored, they miss parties and excitement, or because – vaguer still – they're just not happy. They claim they have less in common than they did, including bed, they don't enjoy each other as much, they're feeling pressured by children. Life isn't fun and games anymore. This is where the scene changes to the lawyer's office.

Statistics prove that a divorce is easier to get than it used to be and it's no longer such a disgrace, though it is an expensive pity. It certainly does cost, and not just the high price of lawyers. Although some reports are exaggerated it is still true that the money gap between husband and wife widens sickeningly with divorce: his income usually goes up and hers goes down.

It might be worthwhile to consider briefly family law and marriage contracts. The laws are changing all the time, as legislators try to keep up with what's happening out there in the divorce courts. Most recently, a law has been passed, requiring that the ex's support payments be taxed from *his* (usually his) income rather than from hers. This is not as equitable as it sounds and, in fact, serves to help only those divorced women who have a decent income and who therefore will save some money on their tax payments. Under the old system, a judge could take into account the woman's income and increase the husband's payment to make up for what she would have to pay in tax. Not that all judges are that careful in their considerations. As for what happens to court-ordered support payments, that's another can of worms.

When a man divorces he becomes single, the saying goes, but when a woman divorces she becomes a single mother. Support payments are noto-

riously low and notoriously defaulted (between 50 and 90 percent, depending on the province). Most of the provinces have established recip-
rocal agreements to enforce payments across provincial borders, and
tougher laws are being enacted, like the garnisheeing of the defaulter's
wages, the loss of driver's licenses, and so on. But with all the government cutbacks, offices that were set up to administer these laws and the
money owed have decreased in number; staffs have been reduced and
the overloaded phone lines, including the answering machines, are busy.
A single mother and her children could be very hungry before her payments come through.

I read a conservative estimate of the amount of money owed in defaulted support payments by Canadian fathers: about 90 million dollars.
Taxpayers have to make up the deficit to support single mothers, and their
children, whose welfare payments have been cut to make up for it.

It's still a winner-take-all attitude in the divorce court and the principals are playing without a net. The no-fault divorce law and the even
split-down-the-middle law, both attempts to redress the painful
stringencies of the divorce system, are still not necessarily fair for either party, particularly in the case of a second marriage's breakdown. In
this case, each party stands to lose half of what was rightfully his or hers
from previous efforts in which the other had no part.

In the case of a first divorce, however, where the spoils may be divided
from a "standing stop" as one divorcée put it, it's like dividing the assets
of a factory, leaving the major income-generating machinery on one side
only. (Even when a woman has a job of her own, she usually earns less
money than her ex.) When the machinery starts up again, the half without it slips back, having no continuing source of significant income, using up capital until penniless while the other one chugs along merrily. In
the past, little recognition was given to the efforts of one partner toward
creating that income-bearing machinery. A scenario from my genera-

tion was so familiar it became cliché, of the wife who put her husband through medical or law school, only to have him turn her in for a younger model after he was successful. Unfair, unfair.

One divorce lawyer I interviewed told me she thinks marriage contracts are unnecessary for first marriages but sadly needed for second marriages, especially if there are adult children who worry about that Other Person getting his or hands on Mom's or Dad's money. Younger children have to be protected as well. So a will, which should be updated every three years anyway, is an absolute must whenever a new union, marriage or common law, is entered.

The division of spoils at the time of marriage breakdown is a crucial issue. The Murdoch case made history and set a precedent: the farmer's wife contested – and won – a property settlement made at the time of her divorce because her years of unpaid work in the home and on the family farm had gone unrecognized and unrecompensed in the settlement. I've already had this conversation about invisible, unpaid work and the GNP.

The Canadian judicial system, being adversarial in nature, is not great when it comes to settling family law disputes. Inevitably, when it comes to that, a lawyer must enter the picture. His and hers, preferably. A woman's husband's lawyer may be a friend of the family, but he (or less likely she) may turn out to be no friend of hers when it comes to dividing property or establishing child-support payments.

Divorce is very expensive from any point of view. I know men who have been paying "alimony" under the old divorce laws for years and years and years, long after the children were gone and it was finally too late for the woman to make a life/living of her own or to get off his back.

But I know absolute horror stories of single mothers living on welfare, in terrible debt, while their husbands continue to enjoy six-figure incomes. These are the situations that caused the expression: "Most wives are one man away from welfare." Intelligent, well-educated middle-class women who thought that welfare was, like death, something that happened to other people – that only poor, unlucky, uneducated or morally questionable women ended up on the dole – can suddenly find themselves in such a box, with no air holes. I worry most about the children. It's too bad there can't be divorce insurance with children as the beneficiaries.

This is not to say that we should eliminate divorce. There are genuinely unhappy people out there who, for the sake of their health, their sanity or their safety should not be living together. Divorce is the best thing that can happen to women who are victims of battering. Divorce seems to be the only solution when one partner is a chronic incurable alcoholic. A mother is doing the right thing when she takes a sexually-abused child out of the reach of her father. In spite of the initial shock and pain, most people emerge from a divorce feeling better. If only the money weren't so tight.

Here is a bouquet of comments from both male and female sufferers, gathered over years of listening to people.

➤ It was like when I had mono – once the fever was over I was terribly weak, but I felt this relief.

➤ I went crazy. I had to have a new woman every night to reassure me I was still attractive to the opposite sex.

➤ I got really sick. All my defenses were down and I got one cold after another. I was a walking zombie all that winter.

➤ I missed someone waiting for me when I got home. I used timers to turn on my CD and lights so there was noise and light when I came in.

➤ I used to lie on the living room sofa in the dark listening to old tapes, love songs, and lie there, not crying, just numb.

➤ I'm not an alcoholic but that first month I used to kill a bottle of single malt every night so I could sleep.

➤ I felt raw.

➤ I was consumed by hatred.

➤ I can't live with him, but I don't know how I'm going to live without him.

Divorce, of course, is good for the economy, requiring as it does two of everything where there used to be one (fridge, stove, dishes, beds, and so on). When possessions are split there are always gaps and overlooked items. Never mind dividing the CDs, who gets the corkscrew? Inevitably the Great Divide causes forays to the stores to replace common household items. But the first thing that has to be replaced is self-esteem. It's called survival.

As a process, survival takes time, but it can be helped along. Creating a new space can be healing in its way, although sad, too, if it is (it usually is) much smaller than the space shared by the family that was. It's important to be nest-like about this new space, establishing a Pampering Place (I'm not talking about diapers), a place to relax with coffee or a drink, and take the time to think – or not. Music is sometimes better than thoughts. It's the ritual that is important.

I, of course, am a great believer in paper, and could not have survived the loss of my love without it. I have recommended its use to many people who were not writers. Paper – foolscap or a notepad or a journal – provides a daily non-judgmental outlet for anger, fear, bitterness, hopes, plans, whatever, and no one has to know or see. I have discovered in the course of my research that many people over the centuries have turned to their diaries to express their pain. It's called recovery.

Friends are essential to survival. So many divorced people have told me bitterly that their ex "got custody of their friends." Others say, as they say after bereavement, "you find out who your friends are." For their part, friends feel awkward too, sometimes feeling forced to take sides, and finding the pressure difficult. One friend, trustworthy and true, is all anyone really needs. Care must be taken not to dump too hard or too often on a friend. As the poet Kahlil Gibran wrote in his book *The Prophet*:

> *...let your best be for your friend.*
>
> *If he must know the ebb of your tide, let him know its flood also.*
>
> *For what is your friend that you should seek him with hours to kill?*
>
> *Seek him always with hours to live.*

Friends change as the living changes. An event as traumatic as divorce (or bereavement) throws a gigantic wrench into the works and changes lifestyle, patterns, needs, and friends. Somehow friends seem to know before the victim does how drastic the changes are and how wide the rift between them is growing, particularly if the survivor is female, I want to say, but I am told I'm biased, having experienced only one side.

Singles of both sexes make couples uncomfortable. The death of a spouse reminds others of mortality, something most people prefer not to think about. Divorce frightens them for other reasons. Who knows, it might be contagious? I had thought that single women were the only ones considered predatory and potentially damaging to others' marriages, but divorced and widowed men have told me that they have been warned off the premises if they spent too long talking to one man's wife. Even close couple friends cannot always find it in their hearts to keep on welcoming a "dangerous" single in their midst.

So it often becomes necessary for newly single people to make new friends. The new broom is going to sweep a lot of things out of their lives, not only corkscrews but also people. It would be wise for them to stop clinging to the past too tightly, because it's very hard to back into the future. For the same reason, it's a good idea not to wallow. Some of those people I quoted offer good examples of what not to do: lie in the dark listening to old tapes, drink Scotch every night, sink into self-pity. Not to say one doesn't need time to heal. But no one has a corner on pain.

One of the best ways to confirm that sad fact is to look around, reach out, and help someone else who is in pain. There's a lot of it going around so there's never far to look.

I mentioned the importance of friends. Ditto, double, for families, sometimes including, surprisingly, one's former in-laws, especially if there are grandchildren floating about. It's hard on grandparents to lose touch with their grandchildren just because the parents have split. If both sides can manage not to cast blame or hurl accusations, they may find in each other another source of love and support, at least for the children.

I'm not just talking theory. I've lived through enough of this myself to know it's true. My older daughter doesn't like highway driving and prefers not to visit me with the children unless she's going to stay a while, like summer vacation. Weekends are out. Her ex, on the other hand, doesn't mind, and he likes off-season activities too (cross-country skiing, snow-shoeing, fall fairs, etc.). So he will come for a weekend with the kids and my grandchildren and I get to visit. I felt strange the first time he did this and I'm sure he did too, but it was okay. We don't sit around in the evening and have deep conversations. We play games with the kids until their bed-time and watch a movie. And I've learned to snowshoe.

Who knows what they can do until they do it? And how do we know where we're going until we get there? In the meantime, there are amaz-ing things happening all around us all the time if only we are open enough to accept them. Being open is an essential part of forgiveness, the abil-ity to let go and move on. No one can live closed up and bitter. It's too damaging.

There's no such thing as no-fault divorce, not really, in spite of the new divorce laws. But there's no reason to dwell on the faults, no matter whose they were. We change, we move on, we grow. Survival is based on change and growth and families need to do both – change and grow.

CHILDREN AND DIVORCE

Tell the child that you and your husband haven't been getting along. Then get to the point slowly and carefully.
– Adrian Kulp, fourth grade,
Coopersburg, Pennsylvania*

There is no doubt that divorce has a profound effect on young families. Surveys are constantly being conducted to find out how far-reaching the effect is, what kind of effect it has on children, of what age, how long the readjustment period lasts, and so on. Divorce is still a huge sociological question mark, and sociologists are doing their best to find the long-term answers. What they also have to do is assess the effect on the larger family, the one surrounding that mythical nuclear one. The returns aren't in yet.

Relatives are affected by a divorce in the family, too, especially grandparents, as I have mentioned. The children suffer from this denial as well. Brothers and sisters of one or the other spouse often become unofficial counselors of the injured parties (both parties are injured), and possibly role models for the affected children. We keep coming back to the children.

A divorced woman told me how happy she was, living with her children in a shack on her parents' property, and everything was going along fine, except her kids kept bringing home strangers for her to marry. The wife of her son's teacher died, and the boy suggested to his

---

* quoted in *Children's Rules for Parents: Wit and Wisdom from Schoolchildren Around the Country*, Harper & Row, 1987.

mother that she marry his teacher because the man needed a new wife and the boy wanted a new father.

"What'll I do?" the woman asked me. We hear lots of horror stories of sabotage by kids, but we also get touching stories of desperate need.

In the long run, I think that divorce must be hardest on the children. If the marriage was so untenable that it had to end, then there is a certain amount of relief felt on the part of the man and woman, to be out of that mess. Any relief the children may feel now that the battle is over – especially if they have been witnesses to terrible fights – is overwhelmed by other feelings, like rejection, guilt, fear and insecurity.

If someone has left, with or without a fight, the child as well as the abandoned parent feels rejected. The child may also feel responsible for the departure. ("Was it something I did?") If the child has been hustled away with the departing parent, there are guilt feelings and worry about the parent left behind. The fact that anyone left makes the child fearful about the remaining parent. If things get too heavy, will that one leave also? Overriding is a terrible sense of insecurity. ("What's to become of me?") The bottom has just dropped out of this corner of the world. The foundations have been rocked. No one will ever be safe again.

That's the emotional view of divorce. In actual fact, family surveys reveal that over 50 percent of the children of divorced parents are indistinguishable from others within five years of the split. The most important item to guarantee their survival is love. Love and place. Still another survey indicates that the place is more important than the personnel in the case of an upheaval in a child's life. Stability counts.

Certainly if the custodial parent is emotionally stable (sometimes that's asking a lot, given a messy divorce), and keeps providing love and a well-structured life, including a stable, i.e. permanent home, then the child's foundation remains secure. And if the non-custodial parent goes on assuring the child of continuing love and proves the claim by seeing the child regularly and by supporting the custodial parent, then perhaps this corner of the world will keep on feeling safe.

The second biggest problem of any child left in the custody of the mother is money. If the standard of living has gone way, way down after the breakup, then of course the children are going to feel threatened, deprived and hard done by with good reason. They are. Life will never be the same again, nor will it ever be as good materially as it might have been. There are compensations. Serenity within the house is one of them.

The financial deprivation shows up most clearly in the levels of education reached by students from broken homes. Another study has shown that fewer adults with high academic achievement come from one-parent homes than two-parent homes. Less education usually means lower-paying jobs, so the deprivation becomes long-term, even lifelong. It stands to reason that good schoolwork is dependent on a stable (quiet, secure) atmosphere, the guidance and attention and concern of both parents, and decent living (studying) quarters. Plus these days it costs. There's always something – a visiting show, an extra book, a school excursion – that requires money. If the kid from the divorced family doesn't have it, it hurts.

The proposal is coming from the schools now that the parents involve themselves more closely in students' schoolwork. I truly wonder if this will help. Parents need time to help with homework – some schools are even proposing assignments for the parent(s) to complete. Time is something both double-income and single parents are short of.

When there's too much noise and too little space, no discipline because no time to follow up on it, and bad food, a kid will go into the streets to find his space, his entertainment, the things he lacks at home. Still other surveys indicate that adolescents with single parents get into more trouble than those from two-parent families, not because of neglect in this case but simply because they've been on their own for too long and they have made wrong decisions along the way about companions, behavior, activities. Peers with similar problems aren't much help. They all feel singular in their lonely, deprived state. Also resentful.

The trouble shows up in the schoolwork first, which is why teachers think they're going to solve the problem by assigning tasks to the parents. If the child, or more likely adolescent, has stopped concentrating, stopped doing homework, started getting more detentions and worsening grades, there's trouble brewing. And the parent often doesn't know. My son John didn't tell me till several years later that he had something like 130 detentions in the months immediately following his father's death. He said he didn't want to worry me. Sometimes, when they can't keep up, or when they can't afford to do what everyone else seems to be able to do (the class excursion, play, etc.), they get defiant first, then aggressive. They adopt a what-do-I-care attitude and try to bluff their way out of their humiliation. They become antisocial so they won't have to admit to their peers that they have problems. Others may become antisocial in another way, hiding in their books and refusing to take part in any group activities. Schoolwork then becomes an escape from reality.

As if there weren't enough to worry about. The hard fact is that, for women anyway, they usually don't stop being a parent even if they stop being a spouse, and they're responsible not only for the physical (economic) well-being of the children but also for their emotional and psychological needs as well. Well, it's not that hard. What it takes is love and time. (Where have I heard that before?) There may not be much money, and time may be in short supply too, but the love should be available. Emotional stability is what the child needs most, the assurance that all is still right with this small world. What matters most is love.

This sounds weak, simplistic, goody-goody and unbelievable. The word, the emotion has been bandied about too freely and like everything else, trivialized by Disney, TV, self-help books and the media in general. We expect moist eyes, a lump in the throat, music swelling up and out as a cutesy solution presents itself. Not so. There are no instant or sentimental answers.

The key word is nurturance. People need nurturing, not only small people but big people as well. Women traditionally have been the nurturers, but men (some men) are slowly learning how to nurture and we're all better off for it. Here's what it takes to nurture.

➤ Showing affection, both verbally and physically.

➤ Building trust, including a respect for each child's privacy.

➤ Doing things together, the sooner the better. (All it takes is time.)

➤ Developing support systems within the family (this takes loyalty and commitment) including relatives outside the immediate family unit (grandparents?).

➤ Communicating. I know I've said this before, but it's vital to emotional health, and if there's anyone who needs to be healthy these days, it's families.

Dorothy Dinnerstein is a psychologist who published an astonishing little book in 1976, the repercussions of which still ricochet around the world of feminism and family. There hasn't been a bibliography worth its weight in books in the last 20 years that doesn't list *The Mermaid and the Minotaur: Sexual Arrangements and Human Malaise* among its titles. The argument works its way forward elegantly like the steps of a gavotte, carefully laying out its framework and statement. The statement may sound very simple but it is in fact revolutionary, and it is this: that men must share in the nurturance of human beings or none of us will survive. And that includes male church leaders, politicians, and heads of corporations and governments as well as village herdsmen, miners, factory workers, clerks, computer hackers and daddies everywhere.

As long as nurturance is looked on as women's responsibility, with no status and no recognized monetary value, society will remain at the same time rigidly sexist and softly vulnerable to disaster. Everyone, including girls and women, needs parents – nurturing, loving parents. If only one hand rocks the cradle, the occupant grows up lopsided. Dinnerstein says that we must break the female monopoly over child care, because "female-dominated child care guarantees male insistence upon, and female compliance with, a double standard of sexual behavior."

Therefore it follows that in the case of divorce (as in all cases) children need both nurturing parents – both parents nurturing – in order to survive.

Custody

> *When I can no longer bear to think of the victims of broken homes, I begin to think of the victims of intact ones.*
> – Peter de Vries

The one sadly reassuring fact about a death in the family is that when it's over, it's over. The surviving spouse gets to keep all the forks and the VCR; the kids know whom they have to turn to. With divorce, on the other hand, the complications are just beginning. After the division of spoils comes the division of the children. It's hell for parents and it sure isn't easy on a kid. Oddly enough, according to another survey, the children of bereaved homes are more likely to have problems at school, especially boys, especially if the female parent died.

In Bertolt Brecht's play *The Good Woman of Setzuan*, a judge has to decide which mother keeps a child of contention: the woman who physically bore him or the one who saved him from death and took care of him. The judge (the story was old when Brecht told it) orders each mother to take an arm of the child and pull. The one who wins this tug-of-war will win the child. The biological mother won't let go; the other one relinquishes her hold rather than hurt the child. The judge then awards the child to her. Judges still play God. The child is still the one who stands to be the most damaged by the split in the family that led to this human tug-of-war.

When that precious scrap of humanity was born, the baby was a miracle, one that both parents (maybe) vowed would be kept safe from tigers. Tiny babies tend to bring out the best in fathers as well as mothers. All the parents' care and tenderness, even ignorant care and uninformed tenderness, is focused on this little link of their union and this fragile hope of the future. We see on television now obscenely young parents who have beaten a baby to death because they couldn't stand the noise. The tragedy didn't begin when they brought the baby home from the hospital; it began in their own families and in the society which failed to nurture them.

It's just as devastating a tragedy, though perhaps not as dramatic or violent, when two warring parties face each other across a courtroom, bitter and determined to get what they think is rightfully theirs, using their children as weapons to hurt each other.

Not that parents intend to use a child as a weapon, not at first, anyway. They want only what is best for the children; they intend to reach some agreement that is least disruptive to the family. Hah. Then someone starts apportioning the money and the time, and then somehow the love is in short supply too.

The reason there are so many female lone parents (80 percent of lone parents are mothers) is that they get custody of the children, in direct contrast to what used to happen before the turn of the century when, granted, divorce was not as frequent and women had less money and fewer rights. A Victorian patriarch owned his children as well as his wife and could easily bar her from ever laying eyes on her children again if he so chose.

Now there is another pendulum swing back from automatic granting of custody to the mother. When fathers do contest now, they gain custody in 74 percent of cases. The good women of Setzuan often give up their child because of the material advantages to be gained – for the child. When mothers are awarded custody and fathers are ordered to pay child support, we know what happens as much as 90 percent of the time. Fathers default, they leave the children and possibly the town or the province (though the laws are catching up with them), start afresh with new wives and children, and forget (or are cut off from) the ones they left behind.

That's one scenario, too cynical I know, but also too frequent. There's another side to it, also bitter. When the mother has the child for all but two weeks twice a year and every other weekend, she has the opportunity to tell the kids her side of the story, a very one-sided side, and often luridly drawn. I interviewed one man in the throes of a divorce who was losing his teenage daughters because his wife had shot him with the Silver Bullet, as it is called now – the false accusation that he had molested his children. It stops a father dead every time.

Even without resorting to that deadly weapon, a bitter divorcée can make unfair use of her unlimited access with the children by poisoning them against their father. Not to say the reverse doesn't happen. No matter whose side the perceived grievance is on, it's unfair (and immature) of one parent to turn the children against the other. All the rankling injustice, all the cruelties and neglect, the continuing shortchanging and wrangling are recounted to the children, dropped like henbane in their ears. It's a wise child who knows his own father, the saying goes, and it was never truer than in a one-sided custody case, only the mother often needs some recognition as well.

This ambush is why some men finally give up. They leave, physically and emotionally, because it's a no-win situation. They have lost their children; their children have been lost to them; they go away to try again with new children. Sad stories abound – we've all heard them – of pain *on both sides*, of cruelties both petty and heinous, all leading to an erosion of trust and love than can never be restored. It would behoove a parent of either sex to remember common courtesy.

In spite of a report that says that 50 percent of children of divorce are indistinguishable from children of intact families five years down the line, that still leaves 50 percent who aren't. The qualifying factors that enable some to be relatively unscathed are difficult to guarantee: a stable environment in a family that just became unstable; security when it just became dependent on a meager, precarious child payment and maybe a small income from part-time work by an overworked, frightened mother; emotional support when one prop is absent and the present one still angry and scared. Not great.

When exclusive custody is legally awarded to one parent, with access rights to the other, the latter can be virtually excluded from the child's life. He (in the past more usually he) becomes a visitor, never knowing what's going on, buying favors with no guarantee of love. At the same time, the mother feels she's the ogre, the one who has to make the rules and enforce them daily, the one who has to scrimp and save and serve the daily portion of denial and discipline. Daddy becomes Big Daddy, heavy-handed with the goodies and far too lenient because, what the hell, it's holiday time and he doesn't see the kids that often so he turns it into a popularity contest. If he's the one who left, he may also be spending conscience money to make up for what he did. Theoretically, he is supposed to continue to be a parent, or to exercise some parental authority and to have some say in the child's life, but too often a summit conference with the other parent ends in war so what's the use? In the short term, the competition may seem to serve the child's best acquisitive interests, but in the longer term kids know when they're being wooed for their favors.

And so, little by little, the courts have come around to the idea of joint custody, the equal apportioning of time and responsibility. There has been a growing recognition of the value to the child of a joint custodial arrangement and even, more recently, of a kind of presumption in its favor. It's a growing fashion and several useful books have been published which attest to it and offer solid practical advice. (See Bibliography.)

Joint custody is supposed to avoid the problems of imbalance or impartiality, to prevent one parent from feeling left out and to encourage the maintenance (illusion?) of co-parenting. Originally, joint custody did not include physical custody or the daily care and control of the child; this was awarded to one parent with generous access rights given to the other. That has changed now. Most cases of joint custody involve the physical co-parenting as well as legal and other decisions concerning the child. The daily responsibility, or biweekly, as the case may be, is shared between the two parents. It helps if they don't live too far apart. There are as many combinations of split time, both weekdays and weekends, as there are families to arrange them. Not only do they vary from family to family, they vary within a family from week to week or month to month, depending on the contingencies of jobs and school. It's hard on the parents, juggling time and people; it's downright confusing for grandparents, keeping track. (Do you know where your grandchildren are?)

In the best of all possible worlds, the loving, hands-on presence of both parents in a child's life is the way things should be (and if not parents, then a significant, loving parental figure). It doesn't always happen. It's estimated now that close to half of Canada's children will live with only one parent for some period of their life before they are 16. This used to happen because of a death in the family; now it happens because of divorce. (The ratio of bereavement to divorce has almost exactly reversed since the 1930s.)

Socially, materially and emotionally, the child is better off when centered in the family of origin. Well, we all know that, don't we? Now how do we go about doing the least damage possible, given all the other damaging factors? The one thing any parent surely wants to avoid is to turn the child into a football being kicked back and forth by these ex-teammates trying to score points for themselves.

If joint custody is just going to become another form of competition, then certainly it's not in the best interests of the child. Alternating week by week or half-week by half-week, and alternate weekends can be confusing, even if the parents are close neighbors (physically, that is). Keeping track of one's underwear and favorite toys in two different homes, let alone coping with the busy schedules of two disparate parents, requires corporate efficiency from a kid who hasn't learned long division yet. The really frightening aspect of such an arrangement is that the children can't help hoping that their parents will get back together again. An illusion of normality and friendly cooperation can actually set up false hopes. On the other hand, on-again off-again weekends, with hot and cold running parents, are also not great.

Oddly enough, though joint custody sounds fair, this too can hurt the mother financially. No support payments are ordered, the thinking being that since the two parents will alternate physical support, each will have a similar financial burden to carry: food, shelter, clothes, medical costs and so on. Many fathers actually profit financially by joint custody orders while mothers lose out. Even if the woman works to pay her side of the commitments, women still get paid less than men, so she is hard-pressed to meet her "half" of the obligations. This is another consideration. A woman must take a close look at the joint physical custody order and ensure that there is a fair division of the financial responsibilities for the children's support with some possibility of her own survival.

One of the main reasons men cop out of support payments is that they get terribly frustrated trying to be a parent when they can't get at their kids. They have lost the currency of the daily exchange, so they can't contribute meaningfully to their children's lives. Their exes deny them any real knowledge of what's going on, hamper their efforts to maintain a normal relationship with the kids and run a damaging P.R. campaign behind their backs. Is it any wonder they give up and go off and start a second family they can call their own?

Is joint custody the answer to keep a father in touch with his children? I've had occasion to see it in action at close hand and I'd say so. It turns fathers into mothers, that is, into nurturing parents, more than they've ever been. They may not dust much (who does?) but they cook and help the kids with the homework and spend quality time with them. Sharing custody can actually mean more *home* work than fathers have ever done before. (Of course, this kind of work is still discounted in the GNP.)

A lot of fathers are not terribly organized when it comes to arranging their kids' lives, but then, neither are a lot of mothers. However, studies show that the mother in a joint custody situation will usually do more than her share when it comes to shopping for the kids' clothes, making and keeping their doctors' appointments, planning their excursions and holidays, and so on. When she doesn't do it, it's the children who miss out and complain, and the father who accuses her of not cooperating.

In the past, the father solved his side of the problem by turning to a relative, his mother, a nanny, or a new wife to do the work for him. This isn't as true as it was. I have seen responsible fathers in action, doing all the things that mothers do, and doing them very well, without calling in the troops. All it takes is experience, and they're getting it.

13

Fallout

Children in general like the company of grandparents.
– Alex Comfort

WHO GETS CUSTODY OF THE GRANDPARENTS?

Grandparents, as I have indicated, tend to get shortchanged or forgotten during/after a divorce in the family, depending on which side custody is settled. With joint custody it's a little safer, that the seniors will see the juniors, because the kids are supposed to get equal time with both halves, but the organization involved is a killer. If there are several divorces and blended families within the larger structure, more grandparents than children are involved and getting to see the kids requires some thought and also a very good engagement calendar. I color-code the weekends to keep track of where my grandchildren are. What I'd like is one of those boards with the sliding counters like they have in hospitals: "The doctor is IN/OUT."

There's little chance of whisking a child or children away for the weekend for a visit because that means that the parent whose turn it is to have them won't see them for three weeks. As for a Saturday afternoon at the movies, the family is usually so busy with their weekend chores, duties, lessons, birthday parties, shopping, renovations and all that it's hard to get penciled in. That's in a family that still functions as a family, albeit separately.

It's still important for grandparents to be squeezed into the schedule, valuable for both generations – children and grandchildren. Grandparents can actually ease the pressure. In his book, *A Good Age*, Alex Comfort comments on this: "In all cultures good grandparenting tends to limit parent-child overexposure, which is particularly onerous in our isolated small-family households." Being an active grandparent is one continuing responsibility of seniors which they should hang on to, difficult as the institution of serial polygamy may make this.

The Vanier Institute of the Family, as might be expected, deals with this aspect of family breakdown as well, exploring the effects on grandparents. Reporting in the September, 1994, issue of *Transition*, Michael G. Cochrane, a Toronto lawyer specializing in family law, says it was never his intention to concentrate on family law, let alone focus so exclusively on grandparents. During his years with the Ontario Ministry of the Attorney General, Cochrane explains, he was frequently contacted by groups such as G.R.A.N.D. (Grandparents Requesting Access and Dignity) and tried to help them obtain access and sometimes even custody of their grandchildren.

Even after Cochrane had left the Ministry, grandparents kept coming to him with ongoing horror stories about the parents: drug or alcohol abuse, psychiatric problems or related loss of control, and even life events putting children out of reach. (For example, one couple's son had died and their daughter-in-law remarried, leaving her late husband's parents bereft of grandchildren as well as their son.) By the time people came to Cochrane in their desperation and pain, private efforts had failed and they were ready to go to Court.

Sometimes the separation of grandparents from their grandchildren arose from a messy divorce or separation and unfriendly custody arrangements; sometimes it came from trauma in the child's life: abuse, psychiatric problems, cults.* Sometimes, sadly, the grandparents simply didn't get along with the intact family and were cut off. In all cases, they seek redress, not monetary, simply an opportunity to be with the younger generation. They have rights and there are legal avenues to follow.

It's ironic, though, that there should be such cases when so many families would give their eyeteeth for a grandparent. I actually saw an ad in the paper, a young single mother advertising for a grandmother. She hoped to exchange services, affection and access to her child in lieu of money. It does work. I have interviewed church groups organized as arbitrary families, comprising members of all ages, people without blood relatives of their own, who celebrate together (Thanksgiving, Christmas, etc.) and who help each other with chores, advice, services. I am told that grandparents are very popular. They're called "fictive kin."

I have mentioned a delightful man I know, too far away from his own grandchildren (and with an unresponsive daughter who refuses to make the effort to bring them together). For nine years he has gone weekly to a kindergarten in his area to read and chat with and tell stories to the children. He has become an honorary grandpa.

It's also ironic that with the shifting combinations of blended and reconstituted families after divorce there are so many parents and grandparents. Extended families in the past were never this big or this complicated!

* I did a reading workshop with a bright, well-prepared high school class one day and found out it was their teacher's birthday. It was a beautiful day, it was an area I was unfamiliar with, it was her birthday, so I invited her for a drink after school and a walk in a nearby park. She told me she was planning to take early retirement and do some writing. I asked her if there was anything in particular she wanted to write about. There was. "I've been a victim of a cult all my life," she said. "First in my family, then with my husband, also a member. I was hypnotized not to remember. I've recently separated and am just beginning to recover my memories." I wonder if grandparents could have helped her?

THE SINGLE PARENT

No one can yet gauge the subterranean impact of a
generation of single parenthood on the lives of children.
– Newsweek

The media are fond of sweeping statements like this, hinting at dire results, with no foundation. Like that *Newsweek* statement that an unmarried woman over 35 had more likelihood of being attacked by a terrorist than of getting married. Everyone snapped after that tidbit, crowing gleefully and pointing at the poor single females who were supposed to be withering on the matrimonial vine. It wasn't true.

So what can we do about the "subterranean impact" of single parenthood on our children? Cope.

Single parents are not a new phenomenon, but they're more visible, they're poorer, and the reasons for their singularity are different from those in the past. In the past, lone-parent families tended to disappear. Widowed women went back to their families of origin and reared their children with the support of their family and community. Or else they remarried and raised a blended family – usually with widowers with children. (There were more widowers around then than there are today because wives used to die so regularly in childbirth.)

Although the present-day causes that leave parents single are more frequently divorce or separation rather than childbirth mortality or war, about one-third of lone parents are still bereaved. There is one other category of single parent: the ones rearing children outside of marriage, an increasing situation today as young unwed mothers choose to keep their babies rather then give them up for adoption, and as older single women choose parenthood without marriage.

In whatever case, these families do not return to their families of origin. Sometimes it's too far to go, sometimes the families of origin aren't there anymore. Whether from need or choice, single parents try to remain independent, rearing their children on (minuscule) widows' and orphans' allowances, or (grudged, defaulted) support payments, (skimpy and getting skimpier) welfare or mothers' allowance checks, or whatever kind of (low-paying) work they can get that will still enable them to keep a home for their children. Eighty percent of all single parents are women and of these, two-thirds of them live below the Low Income Cut-Off. They are probably among the most stressed parents in our society today, and their children the most economically and socially disadvantaged. The majority of lone parents, as I say, are mothers. The picture we get of them is another aspect of the feminization of poverty.

Surveys turn up some strange figures and discoveries. It has been found that in a comparison of the living arrangements of male and female lone-parent families, the women were much more likely to be living without an additional person (other than their children) than their male counterparts were. In other words, the males were shacked up with someone, probably of the female persuasion. Government snoops go looking for shaving supplies in the bathroom of a welfare mother, assuming that if a man is present, she doesn't need the money and is cheating the taxpayer.

Several years ago, when I was investigating the living conditions of an old age pensioner by living on the Old Age Security myself, I used to go to a women's hostel for Sunday dinner: guaranteed vegetables and conversation. I asked the advice of an acquaintance I had made there, a woman living on welfare. I was being "courted" by a man in the rooming house I was in and wanted to know what to do about it. Her reply: "Just don't live common law, or they'll take away your welfare!"

Apart from that deterrent – that is, the specter of losing one's income, however meager, if one had a live-in friend of the opposite sex – a female lone parent is not likely to find someone willing to take on her and her children and her poverty. That's why 75 percent of single mothers are "maintainers," according to the Census – that is, sole supporters living without other adult persons in their households. Aside from the fact that there's no one to share or help out with the expenses, there's no one to help out with anything – with the kids, with the chores, with the reassurance and support and relentlessness of it all. It gets lonely.

Surveys turn up other odd facts. I have already pointed out that single working mothers with children do less housework than married working mothers with children. I have always maintained that husbands are very time consuming (bless them!), but there are reasons to have them around. For one thing, they do go to the drug store at night to get more cough syrup. For another thing, they're good for morale. They may not get up in the night with a sick child, but they make nice comforting noises and seem to worry about it too, if they're awake. (The only time I ever got mad at my husband was when he was asleep and I wished I were.) That emotional support is important.

One of the dangers of being a single parent is that one tends to lean on the kids too much, both for companionship (not bad) and for emotional support (not good). It's nice for kids to have the single parent's undivided attention, which they are more likely to have in the absence of the other parent. But the parent cannot expect the children to fill in the gaps left by the missing spouse. Women, particularly, tend to relate more to their daughters and to treat them like dormitory pals. That's fine, up to a point, as long as they remember this "friend" is still a kid. She is not equipped nor should she be expected to help with the decision making.

Information about how female lone parents relate to their sons, particularly over the age of 16, was not as readily available – for a while. Now, like everything else, it is being dealt with in books and magazine articles, full of advice and anecdotes, heart-warming stories and finger-wagging cautions. The one danger I have observed of single mothers' relationships with their sons is the same as with daughters, for different reasons – that of leaning too hard, and of banking too heavily on the friendship angle. I guess that goes for fathers, too.

I remember a line of the comedian Sam Levenson, reminding his kid who was in charge: "I'm not your friend, I'm your father." It would be a good thing for both genders to remember that. We're still the grownups, so we should try to act like it.

Emotional blackmail in any form, from either parent, is dangerous and damaging. Unfair expectations for the girl-child to become "mommy's little helper" or "daddy's little hostess," or for the boy-child to become the "man of the house" now that Daddy's gone, or "one of the boys" for a jock father clinging to his youth – none of these roles is good for the child. I am reminded of R. D. Laing and those lethal posthypnotic commands. A kid could be saddled for life with a role he or she never asked for.

Male single parents are having a hard time too these days. Suddenly they have had to become nurturers without the training women have had. They're often victimized by sex stereotypes, but they get the same support or sympathy that women do. I'm wrong. They get a lot of sympathy but they get the wrong kind of support. They actually don't get any breaks, financial or emotional. They're expected, after all, to be brave, tough, mature, wise and powerful as well as knowledgeable about the plumbing and a little girl's ponytail.

Parenting and nurturing are not magical skills that belong only to women. If fact, as more men learn to nurture, they're going to change the world. As St. Augustine said, "Give me other mothers and I will give you another world." Fathers can be mothers too. With any luck we will end up with another world.

If only single parents could be paid for anxiety, by the hour, we'd be laughing – only then we wouldn't get paid anymore. We worry so much about our children: their health, their welfare, their happiness, their future. All conscientious parents have these worries, not only single ones. We are constantly questioning, second-guessing, berating ourselves: if only we hadn't done this, if only things had turned out differently, if only whatever. No one can live with if-onlies. That way lies madness.

Raising a child at the best of times is an adventure, probably one of the most important jobs we will ever undertake. Doing it alone is a major achievement.

PART FIVE

REMARRIAGE

14

Remarriage

Yard sale: Recently married couple is combining households. All duplicates will be sold, except children.
– Classified ad

THE SECOND TIME AROUND

Maybe it would be easier to sell the children – not easier for the kids, maybe, but for the new couple. Second marriages are nothing like firsts, and it's mainly because of the kids. They're not to blame, of course. Look what they've lost, through no fault of their own. When a new parent – a step, male or female – comes into the family picture on either side, there has to be trouble, doesn't there?

Anyone entering a second marriage with the expectation that it will be like the first one is nuts. That's a technical term meaning naive, unrealistic, overly optimistic, and nuts. Between 1965 and 1988 Canada moved from having one of the lowest divorce rates to one of the highest among industrialized nations (*Profiling Canada's Families*). That didn't stop people from remarrying, representing, as Samuel Johnson put it, "the triumph of hope over experience." Sadly, even more second marriages fail than first ones – 47 percent of them – and the main reason is trouble with the children from the first marriage(s). The new mate tries to be a parent to the other spouse's children. Big mistake.

Poor second wife! We have all inherited a number of negative cultural stereotypes about her. She is the Other Woman and the Wicked Stepmother. On the other hand, stepfathers are now getting the rap for the majority of cases of child abuse. I must, for heaven's sake, be very careful before I start generalizing.

A second wife polarizes the feelings of the first wife and the children. A first wife will often focus all her resentment and anger on the second wife and try to get even with her ex through the other woman, even though she may not have been The Other Woman. This is where the hard-luck tales about money begin, with more demands for support, suits for back support payments, garnisheeing of wages, attempts to bring the second couple's standard of living down to or below the first family's, all that.

One second wife I heard of took over her husband's two children by his first wife and cared for them in her home for eight years, only to have the first wife sue for eight years' child support at the end of that time. Nothing was in writing but the original legal agreement, so the husband had to pay up, and there was, needless to say, no recompense for the second wife's services. This is the other side of the sad story of the impoverished, abandoned, and very bitter single parent.

As for the children of the first marriage, their jealousy and insecurity are also usually directed at the second wife. Although she may well not be the reason her husband left his first wife, she is living proof that he will never reconcile the differences that split the first union. She is the tangible threat to any promise the father ever made to their mother and and – who knows? – to them. He *says* he will love them forever, but he said that to Mother, too, and look what happened to that promise.

I love the term *reconstituted*. It makes me think of orange juice – and nerdies.

The Blended Marriage!
From frozen concentrate:
Just add TLC and stir.

It is not, of course, that simple. The danger is of diluting it too much. By that I mean that some steps bend over backward to be "nice" to their new spouse's children, while denying to themselves that they don't feel as loving as they are trying to be. Stepmothers often try to bear too much of the load and they become what one woman called "marshmallow mothers" – too soft.

Here's a funny statistic. In the United States, divorced men tend to marry divorced women; in Canada, divorced men prefer never-married women. I haven't figured out a plausible explanation for this one. No matter, for Canadian steps it means there are more than a few surprises in store. At least they have no standards of odious comparison to bring to their marriage. But I wonder if they are more vulnerable to the slings and arrows of outrageous children.

Second wives, I'm afraid, are not without their own little arsenal of weapons and reasons to use them. A second wife tends to feel fiercely protective of her new husband and of their new life together. She is not above trying to sabotage the first wife, the support payments (that she feels she is helping to pay for now), the expectations of other assistance. She wouldn't be human if she didn't feel some pangs of jealousy over the past when her husband was part of another family. What she has to remember is that was then and now it's her turn to be happy – if the kids will let her.

STEPPING CAREFULLY

She wants your heart in a casket.
When she cuts the apple in two and selflessly
takes the sour green half
she's good and glad to see you poisoned
by the sweet red pulp.

– Liz Lochhead

In the past, it's true, stepmothers have had very bad press. Snow White could tell you a story about her stepmother that would make you choke. Hansel and Gretel's stepmother browbeat her husband into abandoning those darling children who did nothing to her but eat. Stepmothers get it from both parties – the wife and the children of the first marriage. Cinderella will tell anyone who cares to listen about her mean old step-mother and miserable stepsisters who left her to sit in the ashes while they sashayed off to that ball. Because stepmothers have been in a no-win situation, today they tend to overcompensate. They try too hard to succeed with their stepchildren and cause a lot of friction in, if not a failure of, the second marriage.

Death used to create stepfamilies; now divorce is the prerequisite. In Cinderella's time, mothers used to die in childbirth. That's why there are so many stepmothers in fairy tales. Those poor, distraught, helpless wid-owers of old remarried because they simply couldn't take care of the little babies they were left with. They usually married widows, like Cinderella's stepmother, and then if they died themselves, as Cinderella's father did, well, that left the orphaned child in a terrible fix. That doesn't happen often nowadays, though I can think of two cases where it did. In both, the child, a teen aged-boy by the time his last natural parent died, left home.

More commonly now the man dies first, leaving the woman to carry on, with miles to go before she sleeps – alone. The average age at which a woman is widowed in North America is 56 and fewer than one in ten widows remarry. So a widow's children are relatively safe from steps. Not so the children of divorced parents. The rate of remarriage among divorced and widowed men is now higher than the first-time marriage rate. Yet men say they think marriage is a trap!

Stepfathers have problems, too, of course, and I'll get to them. But as it stands, more women get to be stepmothers and, by corollary, wicked witches. They never meant to be witches. They don't feel like witches. What they feel like is a combination of punching bag and victim. They're everyone's favorite target.

Surveys indicate that the happiest second marriages are those between two bereaved people, perhaps because there are no living exes lying about and making life miserable for them, but more likely because each person usually emerged saddened but serene from a happy, successful marriage and has full expectation of more of the same. But – another survey – it's supposed to be even harder to be a stepparent after death than after divorce. Why? Because.

➤ When a parent remarries after the death of the other parent, adult children resent it – surprisingly. The children are usually older (though perhaps not mature). On average, divorce affects people earlier than death. Bereaved parents, therefore, are older, and so are their children. Also, because of the age, there are probably fewer young children involved in a second marriage after death than after divorce.

➤ A mourning parent was a comforting memorial. The dead parent could be idealized. By remarrying, the living parent has removed the pedestal.

➤ The longer a bereaved spouse takes to remarry, the more the children don't want a new parent. They're used to the way things are. This is true of children of divorced parents, too.

▸ One or more children of a dead parent may live with the surviving one, even as adults. If the remarriage creates a home in which they feel unwelcome or superfluous, or if they can't stand their parent's new spouse, they have no place to go but out.

If the stepmother is the Eternal Outsider, the stepfather is the Eternal Invader, and his press, if anything, is worse than hers. Neither one is ever able to be part of the history of the first family and is never allowed to understand it or share it – but then, why should either of them want to? I am now more intimately connected with steps than I ever was and I want to dissociate myself from all stereotypes. So do steps. Before anyone is tempted to generalize about a category of human being, it would be as well to consider the individual.

Thus, before I burn all stepmothers as witches or whip all stepfathers as child molesters, let me remember people I know and like who are one or the other gender of step and stop judging them. Life is tough enough without having to fight off a rigid bias or a crippling prejudice. Steps get enough of that from their grafted-on family. Not that the kids can be blamed, either. Through no fault of their own and with no choice offered to them, they have had a new parent thrust upon them. They feel ambushed and powerless and are doing their best to make others feel the same way. Stepparents have to be saints to put up with some stepchildren's efforts to retaliate. The sad news is that marriages have been known to fail because of the stepparent's inability to cope.

Stepmothers in the past had no help and had to fall back on the resources available to them. The Queen had a cookbook with a recipe for apples that could knock you out; Cinderella's stepmom had a will of iron and two sneaky daughters who made life miserable for the kid. This still goes on. But these days, we have professional counselors and family therapists to turn to, and the sooner the better. When all else fails, it's wise to go back to Square One and start over.

Most people wait until trouble starts before they seek help, the theory being, why fix something if it isn't broken? But something *was* broken – a former marriage. Second-time-rounders don't want it to happen again. Some people can work things out without professional assistance if they communicate well. Often, however, there are too many reticences, too much unsaid, too much fear of reprisal to enable a couple to negotiate their differences. The most complicating factor is usually the child/children from the former marriage(s). Steps must watch where they step.

As with other family problems, however, a sense of humor goes a long way to ease awkwardness and anger. So does paper – my friend. (In this context, it would seem to me appropriate to use recycled paper.) The very act of writing down one's problems, hopes and frustrations puts them into perspective. It's possible to review grievances, both real and perceived, without resorting to shrieks and vases, and to sort out an agenda, a program for dealing with them. I used to do this with my husband; I don't see why it wouldn't work the second time round. It's worth a try and it's cheaper than a shrink.

As for the financial problems of second marriages there's more involved than merely drawing up a new will and marriage contract (see p. 170), both essential. Remarriage creates new financial strain, especially if there are child-support payments to meet. Second wives often find themselves working to pay for the first wife's children and understandably feel resentful. Still, children's needs must be met; they are their father's responsibility, after all, and provincial governments are putting teeth into the laws surrounding support payments.

If the second marriage produces children as well, finances may be especially strained. Both partners must be very open and clear about their responsibilities and attitudes and must agree about the dispersal of their assets, with a clear understanding of who is entitled to what.

In another book, Lynne Macfarlane and I advised wives to be sure they owned their husband's insurance policy so that he couldn't change the beneficiary in the event of a divorce and remarriage. Second wives may not think much of that idea, but I can't be inconsistent. I still say it. Both the first family and the reconstituted family have to learn to balance and be reconciled to all the ties that are still such a bind.

Common courtesy.

PART SIX

THE FUTURE OF THE FAMILY

15

Marriage, Coming and Going

If love is the answer, could you rephrase the question?
– Lily Tomlin

In 1970 in *The Futurist* magazine, Jessie Bernard presented a special report on the future of women and marriage. She made a quick survey of experts' predictions over the previous 50 years. With admitted 20–20 hindsight now, I find them interesting and even encouraging.

In 1927, psychologist John Watson predicted that in another 50 years marriage would no longer exist, family standards would be shattered and the child would be out of control. In 1937, sociologist Pitrim Sorokin predicted that divorce and separation would have increased so much that the lines between sanctioned marriages and illicit unions would be blurred beyond recognition. And, in 1947, sociologist C. B. Zimmerman decided that the family was "doomed unless we turned to the domestic style of our grandparents."

Bernard also read the writing on the bedroom wall and predicted the kinds of marital structures that are indeed prevalent and accepted today.

- ➤ Serial polygyny. It's true, men have more wives than women have husbands in a lifetime.
- ➤ Trial marriages. They're called common law now, and even the income tax people recognize them.
- ➤ Group marriages. We went through that in the hippie movement, but they've fallen out of fashion. Too expensive, I think, and as I've said before, women don't like to share kitchens.
- ➤ Homosexual marriages. Very big now. Bernard was right on the button with this one.
- ➤ The production of children by unmarried individuals.

The popular movie *The Bird Cage* puts this in one context. Child mothers, that is, teen-aged girls delivering and keeping their babies is another aspect of this. But the most significant pattern is that of unmarried mature women opting for a baby of their own, by adoption, by artificial insemination, or with the help of a very close friend – for the sake of having a child, if not a husband.

In spite of all the freebies and the availability of professional services that used to be provided by the family, sociologists still suggest that marriage provides two things that cannot compare with scab labor: companionship and parenthood. Both these assumptions could be challenged now, I think, but I'd like to consider them carefully first.

Companionship is a long, slow-flowering bloom that, set in the best soil, will continue to offer pleasure until evening (old age) or the twilight of the gods (death), whichever comes first. Hand-in-hand-into-the-sunset is a cliché based on gut-level truth. Happily married people always say that they are married to their best friend. Their friendship remains the most important thing in their lives and enables them to weather all upheavals, good or bad, because they face them together. Looking into another's eyes romantically may provide a short-term thrill, and we can all appreciate it, but gazing outward together provides focus and reassurance and long-term comfort. By that outward gaze, I really mean a metaphorical one – looking at one's goals – but it's valuable on a simpler level, too.

One widow told me after her first big trip following her husband's death that the magnificent views she looked at put her into a deep depression, "because," she said, "I didn't have David looking at them with me." Sharing precious moments is one of the most important facets of any friendship. With a lifelong companion such sharing has a cumulative effect. I've noticed people who have been together a long time glance at each other and smile at some little happening. There are layers and layers of perception, pleasure, understanding and memory in a glance like that.

"It's easy to make new friends," an old friend said to me, a long time ago now, "but impossible to make old ones." Old friends take time. So do old companions, old husbands, life-companions. They're worth hanging on to.

I may at times sound strident in this book, angry at some of the inequities women suffer both in and out of marriage in what is still a patriarchal society, but I like men. Let it be understood right off the top that I am not talking about men who hurt women or children – or other men, for that matter. But some of my best friends are men. I was married to a kind, funny, magic man, and I still miss him. My father was a real patriarch of the old school, but he also was my very good friend. I have two sons, quite different from each other, and I love them both dearly, and like them, too. I have been disappointed and disillusioned by a number of men, and also dismissed and ignored. Perhaps I expected too much of them because I had such high standards of comparison. I have been disappointed by women too. I do not wish ill to any man, nor woman either. The best men are already nurturers. I want them to go on growing and changing as they must, as women change and grow. The best thing a man and woman can do for their family is to nurture each other. And be friends.

Obviously, a nurturing companionship need not be limited to marriage. I'm not talking about same-sex liaisons, though the same kind of nourishing friendship can and should exist within these unions, too. I simply mean that companionship, one of the items that sociologists think can be supplied only by marriage, doesn't begin or end there. Nature, I have often said, abhors a vacuum. Something else rushes in to replace what has been lost, or else we try to do it for nature. Most people are desperate in their search for friendship or companionship – or company, or something – when it has been lost. Most people are desperately afraid of being alone, especially men.

Men like marriage better than women. On being asked whether they would marry again, the majority of women in a survey said they would not; men said they would – and they prove it when they get the chance. It's not just the creature comforts that marriage provides that they miss, it's the company. To a lot of people, that's what families are all about, so I can't blame the sociologists for thinking so too. Most people need people, as the song goes – someone there. Most people feel that makes up for anything, even the destructive feelings that can happen with families, or the knowledge that it's make-believe (see fictive kin, p. 189). Most people think it's easier to get along with other people than it is to get along with oneself. One of the tricky questions in a self-analysis quiz is this: "Would you like to be married to you?" Most people wouldn't, although they expect other people to be willing to be. So when people lose their parts in the play, or their partners in the dance, they search desperately until they find another one. The main thing is not to be alone.

So what about parenthood? This other essential component of marriage is also reproducible now by other means, as we have seen: by adoption; by default, as in single-parent situations; in same-sex unions; by accident. Parents, too, can be pulled into action to fill that vacuum. Parents,

I think, are made not born. That's why I have hopes for men becoming better parents. In spite of the way we have all been brainwashed, I do believe that parenting is not biologically determined. It can be learned, thank goodness.

In 1995, the Population Council, an international non-profit group that studies reproductive health, released a report titled "Families in Focus," an analysis of a whole bunch of demographic and household surveys from around the world. In the investigating team's studies of parent-child interaction, they found no society in which fathers provide as much child care as mothers, and very few in which they had regular, close relationships with their young children. Fathers everywhere usually earn more than mothers, but fathers everywhere usually keep more for themselves, and after a split, have a habit of neglecting to pay child support – surprise, surprise.

I suppose our experts emphasize parenthood as a necessary factor of marriage because they fear that in the future women will become more like men and invest less in their children. The hope is that men will behave more like women with regard to their children.

Why can't a man be more like a woman?

Now it's time to discuss the future of marriage. Is it really necessary? Is there any other form which will ensure the future of the family? After we decide what marriage is for, I guess we have to consider what families are for. Marriage first.

I could write an entire essay on marriage without saying a word myself: just quote the great and not-so-great minds of this planet on what they thought marriage was and leave it at that. It's odd that out of the hundreds of good lines about marriage I have come across that I should choose the definition of an Ottawa lawyer from an article about marriage contracts. What Douglas Adams realized, in defining marriage as *"essentially an art form,"* is the amorphous quality of marriage. It's an organism that defies being nailed down, pinned and wriggling, to be dissected, sliced and put under a microscope for observation. It is more complex than the sum of its myriad parts; it keeps growing and changing before your very eyes and heart.

Why discuss marriage, anyway, in a book about the family? Because for most of us marriage is to family what legs are to a table. Marriage is for family, though it can be for other things as well; family is not for marriage, though some people don't get married until they have a family. Marriage is the agreement to let a family happen. I pray that it continues, for the most part, to be the agreement to rear that family when it does happen.

Yes, families can exist without marriage, without children, even. Clusters of people who band together for self-interest and self-protection do indeed make up a kind of family, and married people without children are considered families. Families are simply a bunch (or a pair) of people who live together and try to get along. But – and this is why we still get stuck in the biological imperatives and all the stereotyped roles that have their roots in the primordial mud – there is one equation we take as written in stone:

$$LOVE + MARRIAGE + CHILDREN = FAMILY$$

Granted, the love connection is a fairly recent (maybe 150 years old) addition and complicates things. People of other centuries would ask, "What has love got to do with marriage?"

Love – the perceived necessity of, the maintenance of, the fading of and the transference of – has put tremendous pressure on the 20th-century family. That's one of the reasons the doomsayers are wringing their hands and predicting the demise of the family. As for the nuclear family, its future was always unclear. As Germaine Greer said, "The nuclear family is possibly the shortest-lived family system ever developed." Well, we know that now, but we still cling to an ideal, an ideal of family that we haven't relinquished. And I guess love is the reason for it all, and marriage is the means.

Summing up: Is it all worthwhile?

My grandfather married my grandmother when she was 17 and he 19. She died before he did, in her late 70s (young for our family). The day of her funeral he looked at her, so old and white, in her coffin, and said, "Doesn't she look like a young girl – so beautiful?" He turned his chair to the window and gazed out in the direction of the cemetery until he died.

It is worthwhile.

Now, what about the family?

16

What Are Families For?

We need families because otherwise we would have no place to go.
— a small boy named James

It must be clear by now that we're not dealing with stereotypes or fantasies. Today's families are too individual and too real to be the stuff of fairy tales. Yet our whole system of laws, social services and attitudes is still predicated on myth. Why this cultural lag between legend and reality?

When I was married, Father still Knew Best. By the time my children were leaving the nest, Family Ties were strong but both parents were working and the kid (the star) knew more than dad. Now, Murphy Brown is a single mother and creatures from another planet are trying to simulate human relationships in order to try to understand what's going on in families on the Third Rock from the Sun. It's true, things have changed.

Even 20 years ago, less than 40 percent of the population lived in a nuclear family (fewer still in a monogamous one). Now, one-tenth of that number bears any relation to the classic definition of the nuclear family.

We have double-income families, lone-parent families, childless couples, same-sex families (with or without children), grand old families (with or without grandchildren), extended families, and an ever-increasing number of single households. Marriage continues to be popular, in spite of or because of divorce, because there are more second marriages than first ones. If marriage, as the joke goes, is the cause of divorce, then perhaps divorce is the cause of (another) marriage. I seem to find it impossible to discuss family without being deflected into a consideration of marriage. The form, however loosely defined or modeled, has remained a constant source of family over the centuries. If only the players were constant!

Monogamy in marriage seems to be an ideal less practiced than admired, although I have observed that serial monogamy is popular: being faithful to one person at a time, for a time. At one wedding ceremony I attended, the usual vows were followed by this pledge: "as long as we both shall love." That's shorter than life for most people.

Ah, but families are for life. As most people realize, especially mothers, you don't stop being a parent, although some people try, and that hurts us all. No one can walk away from a major commitment such as a child with impunity. We – society, governments, people – keep coming up against that brick wall of a fact. A functioning family is the safest place to keep children until they are ready to face the world and help build a brave new one. If a child's world isn't safe right now, then the world of the future will not be safe for any of us. I know I'm talking middle-class values here, of course, but, as I've said, they have a trickle-down effect.

I am not a doomsayer. (I have happy genes, as opposed to blue ones.) Situations do not necessarily get worse – but neither do they get better without some effort. They do get different. As Elaine Taylor May pointed out (*The History of Private Life*), middle-class family life has always been rooted in social change and deeply connected to the political world. That's nothing to be afraid of. Maybe it's even truer now when religion is losing its hold on families. Technology (i.e., contraception, Laundromats, fast food, etc.) enables them to act more freely, but not necessarily to function well. The bad news is that the political world hasn't caught up with families and what is actually going on in them.

To recap: Families used to be productive units; they became consuming units, then recreational units. Now they have become a means rather than an end, too casual and temporary to offer much reassurance, no longer the "havens in a heartless world" that the writer Christopher Lasch called them. Still, they're all we have. They are, in their now infinite variety, still our best hope of preparing citizens for the world they will inherit. That's still what families are for.

What else?

I keep talking about the future. Present cuts in education and increases in police surveillance are merely short-term, stopgap measures, not likely to take us to a secure, let alone a pleasant, future. Regenerated families will. It is still the family's job to produce loving, caring, socially responsible people who in turn will look after their families in the future. To do this well, we should start a generation ago; to survive we must start immediately. Can families do it?

We hear the phrase *dysfunctional family* frequently these days. We all know what it means by now, but I began to wonder when the word *dysfunctional* came into our vocabulary. I looked it up in my supplement to the compact *Oxford English Dictionary* (the one with the magnifying glass). The word *dysfunction* was first used in 1916 in a medical context, referring to glandular or circulatory behavior. Its use in a social meaning dates from 1959 and the example illustrating its use is a telling one:

> *That it is functional for mothers of young children to go out to work does not mean that it is not dysfunctional for the well-being of their children.*

Whoever would have thought that the *OED* would resort to editorializing? Does that mean that before mothers left to work outside the home, life was *not* dysfunctional for young children? Unfair!

The fact is, women are still trapped by their biological function into taking more responsibility for families than men. As I and others (Dinnerstein, Boulding) have pointed out, the main task of nurturing has been assigned to, and accepted by, women, not without pain and a great deal of personal sacrifice. Nurturance, however, is not specifically gender related. All families need nurturance, equal parts male and female. I know there are some steps missing in my logic – not missing exactly – but I have taken a few leaps and assumptions based on what I've been working out in my argument in this book. I'm still working on what families are for.

Family is a process. Families are for processing people until they're ready.

APPENDIX

Family Workbook*

Well, that's my book on the family. Why don't we pause now and take stock of what we have learned? Here is a fun assessment for the whole family, designed to help you to function not only efficiently but also creatively in the year to come. There's something for everyone here: creative assignments, essays, quizzes, practical tests, money exams, and photography projects. I've remembered the nuclear family, the double-income family, the single-parent family, the reconstituted family, and even the children. So take your time, treat this as another fun family activity, and you'll be fine.

---

* A slightly different, abbreviated version of this workbook has been previously published in *The Globe and Mail*.

FIRST ASSIGNMENT

Create a baby in vitro. Using a petri dish, one egg, 1/4 cup of sperm, an eye dropper, a sieve, and a J-Cloth® see what you can come up with. You may qualify for the Mary Shelley Award.

SECOND ASSIGNMENT

Using 1 kettle of boiling water, 1 pair of scissors, a bottle of rubbing alcohol, a slug of Scotch, a darning needle, and some dental floss, deliver a baby. Be sure to wash your hands first. Who drank the Scotch? The rubbing alcohol?

THIRD ASSIGNMENT

Write a Second Marriage Wedding Song for a boy soprano and two sullen teenagers, using for instrumental accompaniment two combs with tissue paper and Grandma Tucker on the mouth harp. You will find sheet music on the last page.

FOURTH ASSIGNMENT

Create a nutritious substance that people under ten like better than peanut butter. Make sure a three-year-old can spread it.

ESSAYS

1. Define childhood. Be specific. Neatness counts.
2. What factors have brought the family to the point that sociologists say it is obsolete? Analyze. Get the family to help.
3. Which came first, the chicken or the egg? Discuss, keeping in mind that chickens come from broken homes.

How nuclear is your family?

True or false. (Note: this is a generic questionnaire. Truthful answers are expected from males as well as females.)

1. I have been married once and once only.
2. I have 1.7 children.
3. I like peanut butter.
4. I can find my own socks.
5. I know the name of my neighbor's turtle.
6. I have memorized *Where the Wild Things Are*, *Madeline*, *I'll Love You Forever*, all of the above.
7. I always put the cap back on the toothpaste. (Using a pump will not earn you extra marks.)
8. I know how to make brownies.
9. I know how to darn socks (but I don't want to).
10. I know where my children are.

Quiz

Guess who you are. A family quiz to share with your children.

1. Who are you?
2. How did you get here?
3. What are you doing here?
4. Who are all those others?
5. Where did they come from?
6. Did someone just leave the room?

How mature are you as a parent?

Answer the following statements with your closest reaction from 0 to 5:

    0=Never

    1=Almost never

    2=Seldom

    3=Occasionally

    4=Frequently

    5=All the time

1. My children fart on purpose.
2. I enjoy long weekends with my/his/her/our kids. (You may use more than one number.)
3. I'm afraid my children are going to get
   a) frostbite,
   b) ringworm,
   c) hungry.
4. I am not afraid of picking up jeans that are moving.
5. I have never gotten hysterical just because someone ate all the chocolate chip cookies it took me four hours to bake for the Home and School tea.
6. My children's feet smell like roses.
7. I get nervous when my children are silent upstairs (or down).
8. I think my children's cousins are smarter than my children.
9. I have thrown out the following toys on purpose:
   a) drum,
   b) horn,
   c) game with 73 parts.
10. My children can't read.
11. At times I fear my children will never grow up.
12. At times I fear my husband/wife will never grow up.
13. I am never startled by loud noises coming from the family room.

14. I am afraid I will become addicted to Kool Aid®.

15. I don't want to be told what happened today.

16. I would love to have another baby.

PRACTICAL TESTS

1. (For single parents only.) You have a very important meeting with a new client and your child has come down with the galloping flu. All the grandparents have left for Hawaii and the Galapagos. You have no other relatives within a 600-mile radius. You
   a) send the kid to school anyway,
   b) take your child with you to the meeting,
   c) suggest the client come to your home, bearing in mind that the monthly Home Maid clean-out comes tomorrow,
   d) call your ex and re-negotiate custody, arranging for instant take-over.

2. You are ten years old. Plan a homecoming for your father who is coming home from his honeymoon with his new wife.

3. Draw your family tree, and your mate's. Fill in the names from 1800 on. Failing that, do you know where your birth certificate is?

MONEY

1. Discuss the advantages and disadvantages of the two-paycheck marriage in economical, psychological, and sociological terms. Use graphs and any visual aids you can think of e.g. your checkbook(s), credit card statements, separation agreement.

2. a) Balance your budget.
   b) Show how you're going to get out of debt in one year.
   c) Have some sympathy for the government.

3. Without raising your voice, explain and discuss allowances with:
   a) your three-year-old or

b) your 11-year-old or,

c) your mate.

PHOTOGRAPHY ASSIGNMENTS

1. Take three photographs of the same subject – a family with five children – with the diaphragm wide open, using widely differing f-stops. Don't let anyone leave or move.

   Did you standardize?

   Did you eliminate falsifying factors?

   Did you prepare the set-ups correctly?

   Did you keep accurate and complete records?

   Did you maintain absolute control?

   Let's learn to work with light!

2. "The clues to family interaction are planted in body language which is always less guarded than words and shows up quite obviously in photos." (American clinical psychologist Dr. Alan D. Entin) Keeping this in mind, take a look at your family album and consider the following:

   a) Are certain family members sitting close to, or away from, each other in most of the photographs?

   b) Is anyone's expression consistently happy, sad or uptight when he or she is sitting next to a certain person?

   c) Is there a pattern to who does the hugging and kissing, who responds and who doesn't?

   d) Are there noticeably more or fewer pictures of some people than others?

3. Take a camera to your day-care center and spend the day taking pictures (ask permission first). When the prints are developed, study them and answer these questions:

a) Is this a day care you would send your child to? (If you do, would you still?)

b) Are these the kind of children you want your child to associate with?

c) Would you want your child to associate with a child like him/herself?

4. John Berger (*Ways of Seeing*) said, "The invention of the camera changed the way men saw." What did it do to women? Children? Day-care centers?

5. Make a movie of your life. Whose point of view would you like to take? Do you need a zoom lens? Will the film be rated Adult, General, or Parental Guidance?

A FEW TRIVIA QUESTIONS

1. Do you know your mother-in-law's birthday?
2. Who cleans the lint out of the dryer trap?
3. a) Were you a wanted child?
   b) Did you want your child/children?
   (Answer a or b, depending on your age.)
4. Are you complaining?
5. Who is the most grown up in your family?

There you have it, the family workbook to help you summarize and assess what you learned reading this book. Let's hear it for the family!

The following material is meant to address further some of the issues raised in previous chapters.

HELP FOR KIDS

A crisis line was set up for kids in Canada in May, 1989, launched by the Canadian Children's Foundation and funded by concerned corporations. It offers anonymous, confidential counseling information and referral services on such subjects as physical, sexual and emotional abuse; loneliness and depression; school and family problems; sexuality; pregnancy; alcohol and substance abuse; separation/divorce issues; problems of latchkey children; and suicide. The line is open 24 hours a day, 365 days a year, and its services are available in English and French.

KIDS HELP PHONE NUMBER:
1.800.668.6868

An American counterpart can be reached at 1.800.422.4453.

STOPPING VIOLENCE

There are, of course, ways that men can help to end sexist violence (see Chapter 9). Martin Dufresne is a member of the Montreal-based group, Montreal Men Against Violence. He sees it as necessary for men to break ranks with "male solidarity." He offers a list of suggestions to help accomplish this (taken from *Vis-à-Vis*, spring, 1994, A National Newsletter on Family Violence, published by the Canadian Council on Social Development).

➤ Identify and share your resources. Think about what you have to contribute to stopping violence against women. It can be money (tax-deductible), a truck, some time to do volunteer work, a donation of supplies or photocopies. Perhaps you could join a pressure campaign that actively supports non-violence against women and children, or women's equality.

➤ Set a realistic goal and achieve it. For instance, collect $1000 for a women's shelter. Do it.

➤ Get serious about cleaning up your act. Rid your life, your environment, even your heart, of pornography.

➤ Re-educate yourself. The basis for your power is biased. You have a great deal to learn about women. Share in doing the dirty work – you know, the work that women usually end up having to do. Read about and listen to women, especially those you have hurt, and believe them. Be humble.

➤ Challenge men about their power and privileges. Men will want to rally you to their views, their dilemmas, their interests. Never let them use you against women. Expect pressures on you to speak and act "like a man."

➤ Take a new approach to men. Even though they may be ignorant, dangerous or acting in bad faith, men are your lot.

Don't support them by doing nothing.

➤ Get other men to work with you. No one gets anywhere on his own. And please, don't just talk about it, do it!

➤ Just say NO!

TAKE CHARGE!

There are things seniors can do to help prevent the kinds of abuse and exploitation often practiced against them (see Chapter 10). Here are some tips (from *Vis-a-Vis* magazine, in turn taken from an article by Marguerite Chown of the Manitoba Society of Seniors in the MSOS Journal, Vol. 8, No. 12).

➤ Elderly people should participate in social activities as much as possible with friends instead of family members.

➤ They should also maintain independence and self-sufficiency for as long as possible.

➤ It is unwise to bequeath a house or other possessions to relatives on the strength of the relative's promise to "look after you."

➤ Middle-aged women are particularly vulnerable to financial abuse if they have little knowledge or understanding of their financial position.

➤ Husbands have a responsibility to learn self-care: shopping, meal preparation, and housecleaning.

In some families, there may be a younger relative who cannot cope with the frustrations in her or his life. If the elderly parent agrees to let the younger person share the home, it may lead to elder abuse. It would be better for the vulnerable elderly parent to avoid close daily contact with this troubled adult and refuse to share a home with him or her.

How To Hold A Family Council

1. Identify the conflict.
   - First you define it: one side thinks/wants soanso; the other side thinks/wants suchansuch. If necessary, write down the opposing statements on paper.
   - Break down the issues involved and explore them in a calm discussion.
   - Restate the problem as it has emerged from the opposing points of view.
   - Identify your concerns and feelings about the problem.
   - Allow the other side to identify its feelings. This is different from point of view. This is where gut feelings and resentments can be aired.
   - Focus on the future. What will happen if you do this? Or this? What's the worst that could happen? Go ahead and imagine the worst scenarios you can.
2. Communicate.
   - Now is the time to *listen*. No interruptions, no second-guessing, no overruling, no patronizing! Just listen. With an open mind.
   - Ask questions and listen some more. No editorializing, no defending, no arguing.
   - Listen to what is *not* being said. Sometimes the real reasons or the real needs don't come out for fear of hurting feelings, or for fear of reprisals or punishment.
   - Figure out what you can agree on. Search for a common denominator, some meeting ground, somewhere. You both want the other to be happy, also safe; you both want this marriage to continue; you all want to survive as a family.

➤ Be quiet. Stay calm. Don't blow it now. Don't say anything you'll be sorry for, nothing categorical. ("You always..."), nothing polemical ("You're a slob/a lecher/a slut/a bonehead"), nothing shrill (screaming is shrill).

3. Consider your options.

➤ Have a brainstorm session. Try to think of other solutions, compromises, or even a temporary plan of action that might work while tempers cool and you figure out what's going to happen next. Again, no judging. Take every suggestion offered and consider it.

➤ Consider it and be receptive. No one is allowed to say "That's stupid" or "That won't work" or "Of all the dumb ideas."

➤ Offer lots of suggestions and make a list of them all.

➤ Be appreciative. Praise everyone for helping, for taking it seriously, for contributing, for cooperating, for taking the time.

➤ Especially for taking the time. It won't take as long next time. You'll learn shortcuts. But you might want to take the time, anyway, because when's the last time you all talked like this – and listened?

4. Choose a plan of action.

➤ If you can't make up your mind among yourselves, you may need to call in some outside help, someone more detached than you are. Depending on what the issue is, and the people involved, you may require a professional counselor, or perhaps a teacher, your minister or rabbi, a smart (not nosy) neighbor, an in-law (an in-law is someone's parent and loves you).

➤ Try to be objective. After all the preliminary discussion, it should be possible to be fairly objective and to come up with a solution to suit the situation and the people involved.

➤ It's not written in stone. Try it for a week or a month and see how it works. If there are problems, discuss them and refine the solution.

➤ Remind everyone at this point to be fair and broad-minded about it. Remember: you win some, you lose some. Make that give a little, get a little.

5. Come to terms.

➤ Put the agreement in writing. You can include a few whereases if you like, stating the problem, but be sure to be very clear about the proposed solution.

➤ Include a few escape clauses in the agreement, allowing for back-sliding, errors, or obstacles when it comes to adhering to it.

➤ You've put it in writing. If the document is small enough, post it on the fridge door; if not, condense it and put the key words on the fridge.

➤ If you decided on a trial basis – a week or a month or whatever – agree to a review board when the time is up to see how it's working.

The court is adjourned.

Sunday Breakfast

Buttermilk Pancakes

Stir 1 teaspoon of salt and 2 teaspoons of baking soda into 2 cups of flour, add 2 cups of buttermilk and mix lightly. Break two eggs into the mixture but don't stir yet, except to break the yolks. Melt together 2 tablespoons of honey and 2 tablespoons of butter and stir into the mixture, blending well but not too – much it doesn't matter if it's a little lumpy. If the batter seems thick (it usually is), stir in a couple of tablespoons of cold water. Drop by spoonfuls, or quarter-cupfuls, onto a hot, seasoned griddle. Turn once. (They say you should turn pancakes when you can count 12 bubbles on top. Get a child to help with the counting.) Serve with butter and syrup to the family you love.

BIBLIOGRAPHY

BOOKS

Ariès, Philippe, tr. Robert Baldick.
   Centuries of Childhood: A Social History of Family Life.
   New York: Vintage Books, Random House, 1962
—.   and Andre Béjin.
   Western Sexuality: Practice and Precept in Past and Present Times.
   New York, Oxford: Basil Blackwell, 1985

Baker, Maureen, guest ed.
   Canada's Changing Families: Challenges to Public Policy.
   The Vanier Institute of the Family, 1994
—.   *Families: Changing Trends in Canada.*
   3rd edition, Toronto: McGraw Hill Ryerson, 1995

Barreca, Regina.
   Perfect Husbands (& Other Fairy Tales): Demystifying Marriage,
   Men and Romance.
   New York: Harmony Books, 1993

Bernard, Jessie.
   The Future of Marriage.
   New York: World Publishing, 1972

Blumstein, Phillip, and Pepper Schwartz.
  American Couples: Money Work Sex.
  New York: William Morrow & Co., 1983

Bly, Robert.
  A Little Book of the Human Shadow.
  San Francisco: Harper & Row, 1988
—. *Iron John: A Book about Men.*
  New York: Vintage Books, Random House, 1990

Brandon, Ruth.
  The New Women and the Old Men: Love, Sex and the Woman Question.
  New York, London: W.W. Norton, 1990

Carter, Betty, and Joan K. Peters.
  Love, Honor & Negotiate: Making Your Marriage Work.
  New York: Pocket Books, Simon & Schuster, 1996

Chodorow, Nancy.
  The Reproduction of Mothering: Psychoanalysis and the Sociology of Gender. Berkeley: University of California Press, 1978

Clubb, Angela Neumann.
  Love in the Blended Family: Falling in Love with a Package Deal.
  Toronto: NC Press Ltd., 1988

Cohen, Leah.
  Small Expectations: Society's Betrayal of Older Women.
  Toronto: McClelland & Stewart, 1984

Comfort, Alex.
> *A Good Age.*
> New York: Simon & Schuster, 1976

Coontz, Stephanie.
> *The Way We Never Were: American Families and the Nostalgia Trap.*
> New York: Basic Books, Harper Collins, 1992

Coulter, Laurie.
> *A Parent's Guide to Joint Custody in Canada.*
> Toronto: Harper Collins, 1990

Csikszentmihalyi, Mihaly.
> *The Evolving Self: A Psychology for the Third Millennium.*
> New York: Harper Collins, 1993

Danica, Elly.
> *Don't: A Woman's Word.*
> Charlottetown: Gynergy Books, 1988

Dinnerstein, Dorothy.
> *The Mermaid and the Minotaur: Sexual Arrangements and Human Malaise.*
> New York: Harper Colophon, 1977

Doyle, Roddy.
> *Paddy Clarke Ha Ha Ha.*
> London: Secker & Warburg, 1993

Ehrenreich, Barbara.
   Hearts of Men: American Dreams and the Flight from Commitment.
   New York: Anchor Books, Anchor Press/Doubleday, 1984

Engels, Freidrich.
   The Origins of the Family. [1943]

Faber, Adele, and Elaine Mazlish.
   Siblings without Rivalry.
   Dresden, TN: Avon Books, 1988

Fasteau, Marc Geigen.
   The Male Machine.
   New York: A Delta Book/Dell Publishing, 1975

Fishel, Elizabeth.
   Family Mirrors.
   Burlington, MA: Houghton Mifflin Co., 1991

Fisher, Helen E.
   *Anatomy of Love: The Natural History of Monogamy, Adultery,
   and Divorce.*
   New York, London: W.W. Norton, 1992

French, Marilyn.
   Beyond Power: On Women, Men, and Morals.
   New York, London: Summit Books, 1985
—.   *The War against Women.*
   New York: Summit Books, 1992

Friday, Nancy.
    My Mother, My Self: The Daughter's Search for Identity.
    New York: Delacorte Press, 1977

Galbraith, John Kenneth.
    The Affluent Society.
    Boston: Houghton Mifflin Company, 1958

Gibran, Kahlil.
    The Prophet.
    New York: Knopf, 1991

Gingras, Francois-Pierre, ed.
    Gender Politics.
    Toronto: Oxford University Press, 1995

Goffman, Erving.
    The Presentation of Self in Everyday Life.
    London, New York: Penguin Books, 1959
—. *Stigma: Notes on the Management of Spoiled Identity.*
    New York: Touchstone/Simon & Schuster, 1963
—. *Behavior in Public Places: Notes on the Social Organization of Gatherings.* New York: A Free Press Paperback, The Macmillan Company, 1963
—. *Encounters: Two Studies in the Sociology of Interaction.*
    New York, London: Macmillan/Collier, 1985

Greer, Germaine.
    The Female Eunuch.

London: Paladin, Granada Publishing, 1971

Griffin, Susan.
Woman and Nature: The Roaring inside Her.
New York: Harper Colophon, 1978

—. *Rape: The Power of Consciousness.*
San Francisco: Harper & Row, 1979

—. *A Chorus of Stones: The Private Life of War.*
New York: Doubleday, 1992

Guberman, Connie, and Margie Wolfe, eds.
No Safe Place.
Toronto: Women's Press, 1985

Hite, Shere.
The Hite Report on the Family: Growing Up under Patriarchy.
New York: Grove Press, 1994

Jackson, Marni.
The Mother Zone: Love, Sex and Laundry in the Modern Family.
Toronto: Macfarlane Walter & Ross, 1992

Jaggar, Alison M. and Paula S. Rothenberg.
Feminist Frameworks: Alternative Theoretical Accounts of the Relations between Men and Women.
New York: McGraw-Hill, 1984

Kiley, Dr. Dan.
The Wendy Dilemma: When Women Stop Mothering Their Men.

New York: Arbor House, 1984

Laing, R. D.
The Politics of the Family.
Massey Lectures, 1968, Toronto: BC Learning Systems, 1969
—. *Knots.*
London, Great Britain: Tavistock Publications, 1970

Lapham, Lewis, Michael Pollan and Eric Etheridge.
The Harper's Index Book.
New York: Henry Holt & Company, 1987

Lasch, Christopher.
*The Culture of Narcissism: American Life in an Age of
Diminishing Expectations.*
New York: W.W. Norton, 1978
—. *Haven in a Heartless World.*
New York: Basic Books, 1983

Laser, Michael, and Ken Goldner.
*Children's Rules for Parents: Wit and Wisdom from Schoolchildren
around the Country.*
New York: Perennial Library, Harper & Row, 1987

Lenett, Robin, Dana Barthelme, with Bob Crane.
*Sometimes It's O.K. to Tell Secrets: A Parent/Child Manual for the
Protection of Children.*
New York: RGA Publishing Group, Inc., 1986

Lerner, Gerda.
>   *The Creation of Patriarchy.*
>   New York, Oxford: Oxford University Press, 1986
—. *The Creation of Feminist Consciousness: From the Middle Ages to*
>   *Eighteen-Seventy.*
>   New York, Oxford: Oxford University Press, 1993

Lessing, Doris.
>   *Prisons We Choose to Live Inside.*
>   New York: Harper & Row, 1987

Lochhead, Liz.
>   *The Grimm Sisters.*
>   London: Next Editions, Faber & Faber, 1981

Martz, Sandra, ed.
>   *When I Am an Old Woman I Shall Wear Purple.*
>   Watsonville, CA: Papier-Mâché Press, 1987

May, Elaine Talyor, tr. Arthur Goldhommer
>   *"Myths and Realities of the American Family", in A History of Private*
>   *Life: Riddles of Identity in Modern Times.*
>   Cambridge: The Belknap Press of Harvard University Press, 1991

Menninger, Karl.
>   *Whatever Became of Sin?*

New York: Hawthorn Books, Inc., 1973

Miller, Alice.
The Drama of the Gifted Child: The Search for the True Self.
New York: Basic Books/Harper Collins, 1981 (originally published
as *Prisoners of Childhood*)

Miller, Jean Baker.
Toward a New Psychology of Women.
Boston: Beacon Press, 1976 and 1986

Moats, Alice-Leone.
No Nice Girl Swears.
New York: St. Martins/Marke, 1983
(originally published: New York: Knopf, 1933)

Morgan, Elaine.
The Descent of Woman.
New York: Stein and Day, 1972

Morgan, Robin.
*Sisterhood is Powerful: An Anthology of Writings from the
Women's Liberation Movement.*
New York: Vintage, Random House, 1970

Neumann-Clubb, Angela.
Love in the Blended Family: Falling in Love with a Package Deal.
Toronto: Family Books, NC Press Ltd., 1988

Notman, Malkah T., and Carol C. Nadelson.
Women and Men: New Perspectives on Gender Differences.
Washington & London: American Psychiatric Press Ltd., 1991

O'Reilly, Jane.
The Girl I Left Behind: The Housewife's Moment of Truth and Other Feminist Ravings.
New York: Macmillan Publishing Co. Inc., 1980

Rich, Adrienne.
Of Woman Born: Motherhood as Experience and Institution.
New York, London: W.W. Norton, 1986

Rybczynski, Witold.
A Short History of an Idea: Home.
New York: Viking, 1986

Stock, Gregory.
The Book of Questions.
New York: Workman Publishing, 1987

Timson, Judith.
Family Matters.
Toronto: HarperCollins, 1996

Waring, Marilyn.
If Women Counted.
San Francisco: Harper & Row, 1988

Williams, Raymond.
Keywords: A Vocabulary of Culture and Society.
Glasgow: Fontana, William Collins Sons, 1976

Wylie, Betty Jane.
  Beginnings: A Book for Widows.
  Toronto: McClelland & Stewart, 1997 (fourth edition)
—. *Successfully Single: How to Live Alone and Like It.*
  Toronto: Key Porter Books, 1986
—. with Lynne Macfarlane.
  Everywoman's Money Book.
  Toronto: Key Porter Books, 1995 (fifth edition)

Brochures, Pamphlets, Newsletters

The Advisory Committee on Children's Services:
>   *Children First: Report of the Advisory Committee on Children's Services.*
>   (Ontario, 1990)

Canadian Advisory Council on the Status of Women:
Cantrell, Leslie. Linda D. Meyer, ed.
>   *Into the Light: A Guide for Battered Women.*
>   Edmonds, WA: The Chas. Franklin Press, 1986

MacLeod, Linda.
>   *Wife Battering in Canada: The Vicious Circle.*
>   Ottawa: 1980
—.   *Battered but Not Beaten.*
>   Ottawa: 1987

Canadian Council on Social Development:
>   *The Canadian Fact Book on Poverty.* 1989

>   *Vis-à-Vis.*
>   A National Newsletter on Family Violence published by
>   Canadian Council on Social Development
>   Box 3505 Station C
>   55 Parkdale
>   Ottawa ON K1Y 4G1

Health Canada:
  Seniors Info Exchange.
  Published by the Division of Aging and Seniors:
  Health Canada
  Postal Locator 4203A
  Ottawa ON K1A 0K9

United Nations Children's Fund (UNICEF):
  The State of the World's Children 1990

Statistics Canada:
  Canadian Social Trends.
  A quarterly magazine making sense of Canada's statistics
  published by:
  Minister of Industry and Science
  Statistics Canada, Marketing Division
  Sales and Services
  Ottawa Canada K1A 0T6

  Lone-Parent Families in Canada. Ottawa: 1992

  Perspectives on Labour and Income. Ottawa: Autumn, 1996

  Women in Canada: A Statistical Report. (third edition) Ottawa:
  Minister of Industry, 1995

THE VANIER INSTITUTE OF THE FAMILY

Baker, Maureen, ed.
    Canada's Changing Families: Challenges to Public Policy.
    Ottawa: 1994

Boulding, Elise,
    "Learning and the Familial Society: The Place of the Family in Times of Transition; Imaging a Familial Future." Ottawa: 1981

    Canadian Families in Transition (booklet, different editions,
      regularly updated)
    Canadian Families: The Vanier Institute of the Family
    Canadian Families (1991)
    Canadian Families (1994)

Meston, John.
    Child Abuse and Neglect Prevention Programs.
    Ottawa: 1993

    Profiling Canada's Families. 1994

    "Tell Me About Your Family," *in Learning and Study Guide in Recognition of the International Year of the Family.* 1994

    Transition.
    Published quarterly for distribution to members of
    The Vanier Institute of the Family
    94 Centrepointe Drive
    Nepean ON K2G 6B1

Articles

Armstrong, Jane, Rita Daly, and Caroline Mallan.
Series on violence published in *The Toronto Star* March, 1996, with
follow-up in November, 1996

INDEX